UNTOUCHABLE:
The Cocktail Party
(Part 1)

Siri's Saga
Book 1

by

Jessika Klide

COPYRIGHT PAGE

May you dance through life
with lots of love
and more than a few
happy endings!

PRELUDE

"Moore speaking. Yeah, Sam. I'm checking on them for you. I'm at Dogwood Court now. What the fuck? Let me call you back." *I can't believe it!*

I stare from the cab of my truck at the most beautiful girl in the world as she casually walks across the parking lot, right in front of me. *She IS simply stunning!* My eyes follow her, like a hawk hunting its prey. When she drops her keys, then bends over to retrieve them, I laugh out loud at the view she flashes me. "Perfect!"

The word jolts me. *Perfect.* Unable to take my eyes off her, I watch as she gets in her car. She looks my way before she pulls out. *She is gorgeous.* As she vanishes out of sight, my gut tightens.

Leaning back, I close my eyes and think about what just happened. *What are the odds that our paths would cross right here, right now? They are truly astronomical!* I sigh. *She just walked by!*

I open my eyes and stare at the ceiling. I hear my Grandpa Moore's voice. "Your grandmother completes me, son. She makes me whole." *What if she is perfect for me?*

I sit quietly, thinking about all the possibilities with her *by my side. Could this beautiful, stunning, gorgeous girl be the one that makes me whole? Could she be the one I can honestly share my secrets with? That will understand me, get me, complete me?*

I don't know. I turn to stare out the window. *But what I do know is that an extraordinary opportunity has just fallen in my lap. Only a fool would let it go and I'm no fool. She is not untouchable and I'm going to find out if she is the one.* I open the truck door and get out. *I know what I have to do.* "I have to win her heart."

I call Sam as I walk to the apartment building. "Sam. Moore here. Change of plans...."

CHAPTER ONE

What is it about express lanes when I am in a hurry? It's Sunday morning in Alabama. No one is supposed to be in here. I roll my eyes to the sky, tapping my foot, working on my patience and failing miserably. *I miss Vegas and its 24/7 life style. At least you know the express lanes are going to be slow, no matter what day of the week or hour of the day.* I take a deep breath and sigh. *Don't sweat the small shit, Siri. It's only for a couple more weeks, then you'll be back in Vegas and missing the slow lifestyle of LA, Lower Alabama.*

I pull my iPhone out and check the time. It's 10:40. *Twenty minutes is cutting it close. Finally!* I slide my items up the belt. *You can make up time on the road, no problem. Ok, breathe in ... exhale, smile sweetly.* "God bless you too, ma'am."

Once in my car, I hit the gas. My Ford Shelby GT500 leaps out of the parking lot and the speed relaxes me. *I love my fast and furious ride!* I maneuver through a few cars on the road, then it's clear sailing. Punching it, I let my mind drift to the dance routine I have been working on. I tap the steering wheel to "Happy" and review the arm motions of the opening sequences.

Cat's gonna be surprised when I tell her I want to do a routine as a man. I can hear her now. "Pharrell Williams? 'Happy?' Really?"

"Really."

"But who am I to question you. Everything you do turns to gold. But 'Happy?' That's a tough one. Baby Girl, if you can pull it off, it will be killer wicked for a return performance!"

"If? You know I will bring down the fucking house!" I'll text Cat as soon as my meeting with Mrs. Smith is over. She will be stoked when I tell her I'm coming back.

The weather is beautiful today. I double tap my iPhone. "What's the temperature today?"

"Siri, the temperature today is warm, 75 degrees." *I might sunbath on the balcony later.*

My mind is clear by the time I turn into Dogwood Court at 10:50. Parking in my usual space, I see a 'bad ass' Tuxedo Black Metallic 2014 Ford F-150 SVT Raptor Special Edition 'Real Man Truck' in the visitors spot. *Oh man! What a sweet ride!*

Gathering my grocery bags, I admire it as I race alongside, heading to the front door. *Now, there's a man after my own heart!*

Pushing the door open with my back, I trot-run across the lobby floor. Glancing at the office, I see Mrs. Smith talking to a young man. That quick glimpse tells me, he is athletically built, 6' tall plus or minus, 200 pounds maybe, wearing a pale yellow J Crew shirt with distressed blue jeans. My instant impression is *Hunk*! I rush in the open elevator, whip around, press 9, then hone in on the man target as the doors immediately begin to close.

He looks to be my age. He has a military style haircut. Dark sides and roots but the top is long, thick, golden blonde. It's streaked with natural sun highlights, reflecting the lighting. It's straight, sleek, smooth and moving gently as he talks. Umm. He turns to look at me as the doors close. Our eyes lock and his gaze pierces my core. *OH!* The rest of my view falls away. My heart stops and my breath catches in my throat. When the doors touch, and the connection is broken, my heart jolts and I gasp. Riding the elevator up, my heart pounds wildly in my chest. *Sweet Zeus! What just happened? I'm not sure!* I put my hand on my heart. *Calm down, Siri! Breathe. Fuck, he is fine, but his eyes. Woo!*

The elevator stops on the 9th floor. I run-trot to my apartment on the end, 9A. Once inside, I stuff my grocery bags in the refrigerator, then rush back out. *Hurry. Hopefully, the stud will still be there.* Pressing

11

the down button, I pace. The elevator is slower than usual. *Church is out.* When it arrives, it dings and I rush in. There are four middle aged women on board in their Sunday best. "Good morning." I cheerfully offer their sour puss expressions. None of them speak. They simply ignore me. *Southern hospitality doesn't apply to everyone, I guess.* I tap my foot. *Hurry! I've got to check that guy out!*

Right when we reach the lobby, my iPhone alarm goes off and "Sexy and I Know It" by LMFAO blasts us. "Oh, excuse me." I apologize to the uppity bitches who glare at me, while I reach in my front pocket and the doors open. They exit with their noses in the air. Digging for it, I follow the last woman out. *Dang, it slipped down deep.* The bulky case hangs on the pocket hem and I look down as I blindly walk forward, struggling with it. *What the ...? Come out of there!* I snatch hard. *Oh no!* It releases before the pull and the iPhone slides out smoothly with momentum, sailing past the tips of my fingers.

I watch helplessly as it flies over the head of a young girl texting, blindly walking straight at me into the elevator. *Oops!* Spinning and twirling away, the dancer in me takes over. I manage to avoid a crash, but I dance right into a wet spot on the floor behind a sign saying "Caution Wet Floors." *Ooh!* Sliding in my wedge high heel sandals, I back pedal until I gain my balance. Thankfully, the dancer again manages to avoid another crash. Regaining my composure, I take a deep breath, then glare at my iPhone laying on the floor. It's still blasting the atmosphere with LMFAO.

Walking over to it, I examine my shirt. My halter top has stayed faithful. The key hole shows only cleavage. No nipples. *Well, that's a good thing.* Straddling my phone, the dancer bends over at the waist to pick it up and half my thick, long, blonde hair slips out of the clip, falling in my face, blocking my view. *Great!* With my butt in the air, I release the rest of my mane, letting it engulf my whole face. Then flipping it up and over, I drop my ass, bouncing gently, and quickly twist and re-clasp it on top. Standing, I ask Karma. *What else?* The song is almost over when I finally grasp it. *Yeah! Yeah! Yeah! I'm sexy and now everyone knows it!* Turning it off, I make my way to the office, as if nothing in the world out of the ordinary just happened.

When I lift my eyes to see where I am going, I stop dead in my tracks. My heart and my breath collide in my throat. The stud is leaning on the threshold of the office door completely relaxed, watching me. Our eyes lock. His gaze pierces me. The rest of my view falls away, again. *Oh ... Holy Hades!* Looking at me is a pair of the most gorgeous green eyes, with the most intense gaze, on the most handsome face of the most beautiful man, I have ever laid eyes on, and he has the most beautiful smile on his face. *SWEET ZEUS! He looks like a Golden God!* My tummy lurches so hard it feels like a back flip, jolting my heart out of my throat and releasing my breath. I gasp as my limp fingers drop my iPhone, and I lay one hand on my tossing tummy and one on my wildly thumping heart.

He smirks when my iPhone falls, then grins at my posture. He pushes off the wall and towers over me, still holding my eyes captive. "Hi."

I take a deep breath, then exhale as a smile spreads slowly over my face. "Hi."

Fussing about Ray, the new janitor who left the floor wet, Mrs. Smith comes bustling out of the office. The gorgeous man moves to the side, not letting my eyes go. I stare at him as Mrs. Smith addresses me. "Miss Wright, I need to show this patient young man the available apartment first. He's been waiting almost an hour to see it."

I respond in a voice barely above a whisper. "Perfect!"

"I will meet you back down here in 30 minutes, if that's alright with you?"

"I'm not going anywhere. Take your time."

"Thank you, honey. That's awful sweet of you."

"No problem. I can go up and put my groceries away."

She turns to the gorgeous man. "Mr. Moore, I can show you the apartment now." He looks at her, breaking our connection, and nods. She pats my arm as she passes me and I pull my eyes off him to look at her. She raises her eyebrows twice at me, then winks, and turns back to him. "This way, Mr. Moore." She walks off to the elevator.

He follows her, not looking at me, but when he reaches my side, he invades my personal space and kneels. His body almost touches mine as he slides down. I feel his electric aura. My tummy lurches hard again as I watch his golden hair sway softly when he reaches for my iPhone. *The golden highlights are glittering.* When he turns his face to look up at me, I'm stunned! *His eyes are emerald green! Bright emerald green!*

"I believe you dropped this… again." His voice is deep and sends shivers all the way down to my toes.

"I believe I did." I look away from his eyes to see my iPhone cradled in the palm of his hand. He rises the same way he went down, almost touching me. He towers over me and I can feel him standing there, like static. *Amazing!* Reaching for my phone, I feel a tickling tingle when my skin touches his. *Ooh.*

He cups my hand, forcing me to turn my face up to his. I look into his unbelievably beautiful eyes. "Thanks, Mr. Moore."

He smiles and my heart melts. "You're very welcome, Miss Wright." He backs away, holding my hand until they pull apart. Then he turns and walks off to join Mrs. Smith in the elevator, leaving me standing there staring after him, completely enchanted and breathless.

Watching his retreating physique, I admire his manliness. *His shoulders are very broad. His waist is very small. His legs are straight. His posture is perfect. His gait is strong. He glides with masculine grace.* I watch his ass moving in his jeans. *It is to die for!* My mouth waters.

Mrs. Smith leans around his torso so she can see me. "Aren't you going up too? Come on. You can ride with us."

That puts my feet in motion.

He turns, smiling at me and waits. *Just a little tease for you, Mr. Moore.* I walk-trot up the short distance to him. His eyes watch my bouncing tits. When I'm even with him, he gestures to me. "Ladies first."

My eyes twinkle at him as the dancer glides by. *Teasing is what I do best.* I feel him follow me. Knowing he is watching my ass, I slow down and strut my stuff. *My ass is to die for too.* When I walk past Mrs. Smith, I wink at her. "Thank you."

She smiles. "You're welcome, dear."

Entering the elevator, I move to the back wall and Mr. Moore comes to stand beside me. We stare straight ahead like polite strangers do but when Mrs. Smith reaches out to select the floors, our eyes are locked on her hand. We watch as she only pushes one button, #9. We both smile, staring at the opposite wall.

As soon as the elevator starts to rise, I can feel my temperature start to rise too. His rock hard body is radiating heat, spreading to mine, making me hot. *I know that body is chiseled under those clothes. His chest, his abs, his....*

"It's awfully warm in here." Mrs. Smith interrupts my vision. "The air conditioning must be broken." She takes her phone out to text Ray.

I almost laugh, but I manage to only bust a big grin. Cutting my eyes at Mr. Moore, I see he has shifted his shoulders to watch me. *He isn't smiling.* My grin falls off my face as butterflies start flying wildly in my gut. The intensity of his expression makes my chest grab my breath. He continues to watch me as I stare forward, struggling to breathe normal under his scrutiny. *I can feel his eyes devouring me.* My nipples harden and push against

17

my top. His eyes fall to them. The butterflies soar to the tips and I lick my lips. That makes him grin. As I stand there allowing him to study me, he makes a soft moan within his throat, like a hum. My eyes smile. *I know the effect I have on men.*

When we reach the 9th floor, Mrs. Smith exits first, turning to the right. "This way, Mr. Moore."

He waves me forward and I glide out, turning left toward my apartment. I hear Mrs. Smith blabbing about the furnishings that are included as they walk down to the vacant apartment, 9G, at the other end of the hall. I pace my steps to arrive at my door at the same time. When I hear her jingle the keys, I look down the hall. As soon as he arrives, he looks back to find me. She enters the room and her voice fades, but he stands outside watching me. *Yeah, baby! He is totally captivated.* I open my door and flash him a grin. I see him grin as he follows Mrs. Smith in.

When the door closes behind me, I lean against it and bust into giggles. *This guy has IT! Whatever IT is, he has IT in droves! Fuck the groceries!* "See You Again," by Miley Cyrus starts running in my head. I rush to the bathroom to check my face, my hair, and my cleavage. My reflection smiles back and I see a young girl looking at me. My light, crystal green eyes are twinkling like crazy! My tan skin is rosy from my pounding heart, but I pinch my cheeks anyway and bite my lips too. I release my natural light blonde hair that is heavily streaked platinum, and comb my fingers through it, fluffing it for a sexy tousled look. I survey my face for the trillionth time in my life and smile. *You know you have IT too.* I give myself a wink and reach into my shirt to adjust my tits for maximum effect. *Play your assets.*

Returning to the door, I listen for their voices. When I hear Mrs. Smith, I casually exit. As I pull my door closed, she waves. "Come on, Miss Wright. We will wait for you again."

I turn to see Mr. Moore standing beside Mrs. Smith with a smile on his face. *Umm hmm, he was hoping I would ride back down with them.*

When our eyes meet, he says, "Perfect."

Giving Mrs. Smith a small wave of acknowledgement, I lengthen my stride so that my tits sway gently to the rhythm of my gait. *Work it, Siri!* I am rewarded to see his eyes fall to watch them. *All men love bouncy tits.*

When I reach them, I avoid eye contact with Mr. Moore letting him continue to study my face and my tits. Mrs. Smith is busy texting someone, but walks over to stand next to me. I watch her as I try to deal with the butterflies pushing at my nipples. She looks at me and smiles, then walks a few steps away to text in private. Moore's continued stare makes me shift my stance, and I'm unable to resist his eyes. I look into his face. His eyes are soft and sincere. Mrs. Smith walks back over. "Miss Wright, allow me to introduce you to Mr. Moore. He has decided to rent 9G. Mr. Moore. Miss Wright." She turns away to push the elevator button and looks at an incoming text.

"Mr. Moore." I hold out my hand, "welcome to Cloud 9." I watch his beautiful golden hand take mine. *His touch is tender.* He steps too close again and rolls my hand so the back is facing up. He smiles down at me and holds it. *Are you going to kiss it?* He gently strokes the top with his thumb, sending a wave of electricity though me. His expression makes my tummy do a back flip again and the butterflies flutter. *He is definitely seducing me! It's working too!*

Mrs. Smith puts her phone in her pocket and laughs. "I've never thought of that. Cloud 9. That's very clever, dear."

The elevator arrives with a ding. Mr. Moore strokes my hand again with his thumb, then turns and says, as he motions to the elevator. "My lady." It sounds more possessive than a title.

I'm called a lot of things, but lady isn't one of them. I like the way it makes me feel.

Following Mrs. Smith in, I move to the back for the 'hot' ride down. Mr. Moore follows me in and stands too close. Our arms touch. Instantly, my skin starts to sing. I try to focus on Mrs. Smith hitting the L for lobby, but all I can think about is his rock hard body under his yellow J crew shirt and distressed jeans, and whether or not he wears boxers, briefs or any underwear at all.

As soon as the doors close, he shifts his shoulders to study me again. I stare straight ahead, smiling at the door. After a few moments, I cut my eyes to see his expression. He is smiling too. *Damn. He is fine!* As we travel down several floors, his gaze never waivers. *It feels so fucking good!* I lick my lips several times.

Mrs. Smith remarks again about the air conditioning needing to be checked then apologizes to us for the heat. "It's fine, Mrs. Smith. I'm actually enjoying it."

Mr. Moore chuckles at that.

More of that, please! That was music to my ears.

The silence in the elevator is broken by my iPhone timer. "Wild Thing" sung by The Troggs plays. I bust another grin and cut my eyes at Mr. Moore to find his eyebrows are raised in complete surprise. I give him a flirty look. *I'm full of surprises.* Then laughing, I decide to let it play. *I know this is totally inappropriate behavior for strangers, but fuck that!* The dancer in me taps my heel and my hips thump to the beat as the lyrics describe how I want to move him, make him sing, make love to him and let me make everything "groovy!" On the last chorus, I devour him with my eyes slowly moving from his feet to his face, taking my hands, sliding one to my pussy and one into my pocket to retrieve my phone. I'm rewarded with hooded eyes and an involuntary half smile. *He's thinking, "I like the way you're thinking."*

Mrs. Smith glances over her shoulder. "That must be someone significant."

The spell I cast on him is broken, so I drop my eyes to my pocket to make sure the case doesn't hang on the hem again. When it's free, I turn it off and shove it back down.

Mrs. Smith has continued talking. "I haven't heard that in years. That song was a hit when I was little. Wow! That brings back memories. " She proceeds to fill the air with blah, blah, blah.

Swinging my hair to the side, I look up at Mr. Moore to flirt, but he isn't looking at me now, and he doesn't look at me. He's facing forward like the polite stranger he really is.

He's frowning. My heart sinks. *What's wrong? Why aren't you looking at me? Why are you frowning? Was I too aggressive? Did I come on too strong? Did I turn you off? Shit!* I face forward too and stare at the door. *Siri! You're not in Vegas! He probably thinks you're a whore and wants no part of you now. Shit!* My chest starts to hurt. *I can't wait to get out now! Once you're labeled a whore, there is no going back.*

As soon as the doors open, Mrs. Smith exits. I take a step to follow, but Mr. Moore reaches out and lays his hand on my arm, touching it gently but firmly, sending goose bumps running up my shoulder.

Looking at his beautiful hand laying on my arm and feeling that instant wave of tingling sensations from his touch, I know the depth of what his rejection would truly mean to me. *Real loneliness.* I take a deep breath and contemplate his hand on my arm. *Your skin is a beautiful, sun kissed golden color, and the light reflects gold highlights from your dark blonde hair. You are absolutely gorgeous! And I know gorgeous! I see the best the world has to offer. And you are more than that!*

He strokes my arm with his thumb and I lift my hopeful face to his. "*Is* there someone significant?" His voice is soft and soothes me.

Relief floods over me and I drop my eyes to look at his hand again. *Oh! That was the problem! Mrs. Smith put that thought in your head.* I take a deep breath and slowly exhale. *Does that mean you were scared I wasn't available? Really? After my blatant flirting?* A thought occurs to me. I look out to the lobby as I ponder it, watching Mrs. Smith walk across the lobby floor. *A man like you would rarely be turned down by any woman, available or not. I can only imagine the number of women you have seduced.* I look back at his hand on mine, and he strokes me again, sending goosies up my arm. *And yet, here you are* asking *if there is someone significant. Why?* I lift my face back to his and look directly into his eyes. He holds them captive, searching for my answer, so I tell him before I speak. *You are the most beautiful man I've ever laid eyes on! Ever! Do you know that you make my body tingle from head to toe? Of course you do. You get that all the time. But what makes you* ask *if there is someone significant? Why does it matter to you? You could have me anyway. Oh, you don't share. Of course you wouldn't. You are a dominant male. An Alpha male. A real man!*

I look back out at the lobby and he strokes my arm again. In that same soft, soothing tone, he asks. "In *your* life?" Watching Mrs. Smith talk to Ray allows me time to absorb what he means by that. *Why would it matter to you if I had someone special if I was willing to hook up with you anyway?* I look back down at his hand as it dawns on me, then I look up into his sincere face and give him a sexy smile. *Why were you seducing me so aggressively? Am I the most beautiful woman you have ever laid eyes on? I've been told I'm an exceptional beauty.*

His eyes smile.

Does my body turn your body on like never before? I take a small step closer to him.

His breathing changes ever so slightly.

Do we share an unusual physical connection? I cover his hand with mine.

He closes his eyes.

Do you feel it too? I stroke his skin with my thumb.

He opens his eyes, looking directly into mine and gives me a 'sexy as hell' smile.

You do! My heart jolts awake. Happiness floods my body and I drop my face overwhelmed. *Is there someone significant? Not no, but Hell No! Never! Not until....* My eyes start to twinkle. I tip my head letting my hair hide my face from the lobby. Looking up at him through my eyelashes, I give him my sweetest smile. My voice is light and flirty when I finally answer. "Not until an hour ago." He rewards me with his big beautiful smile and chuckles. The warmth of his reaction spreads over my face. I lift it and stand to face him fully, toe to toe. "And you? *Is* there someone significant in your life?"

The elevator doors close on us. He closes the remaining small gap between us and my body comes alive. The static has turned into electricity. The world shrinks to only his body inches from mine. He drops his head, puts his mouth next to my ear, and says in a quiet voice that washes over me from my head to all ten toes. "Not until about an hour and 5 minutes ago."

And 5 minutes ago? I blink with his words, frowning. *Oh! You're talking about my iPhone toss, my near collision, then the wet slide, my hair flop and drop, finally rescuing and turning off my phone, only to drop it again because you are so damn, drop dead, gorgeous.* I blush beet red embarrassed. I hide my face in my hands, shaking my head. "I must have looked like the biggest goofball ever!" I peer over the tops of my fingers at him. "Can we erase that 5 minutes, please?"

He laughs at my expression and the sound is infectious. I giggle as he taps his head. "Nope. Steel trap."

The elevator doors open again, and we exit laughing. We walk together to the office where Mrs. Smith is patiently waiting for us and Mr. Moore asks me. "So, who *is* the Wild Thang?"

I start to giggle again. "No one. It wasn't a phone call at all. I set my timer earlier to make sure I didn't get trapped in the office listening to Mrs. Smith tell stories about her cats."

He laughs out loud at that. My heart sings with the sound of his happiness. He says with the correct voice inflection from the song. "Groovy!"

I crack up with that.

When we walk up, Mrs. Smith smiles at us both. "Well, it looks like you two have hit it off." Neither of us comment, we just smile at each other. "Mr. Moore, I'll have the paperwork drawn up tomorrow."

"I'll see you then." He answers her, then he turns to face me and says softly so only I can hear. "I hope to see you tomorrow too, Miss *Wright*."

I look one last time for today, into those gorgeous, emerald green eyes, and drink in that gorgeous, golden face. I whisper. "Ditto, Mr. *Moore*." He smiles, then turns and walks away. I admire the view as I watch him walk out the door to the big 'bad ass' Ford Raptor Special Edition 'Real Man' Truck. *Yes, of course, that is* his *ride. Definitely a man after my own heart.*

I turn back to Mrs. Smith. She has been watching me watch him. "He is quite the handsome young man, isn't he?"

"Yes. He is."

When we go inside the office, there is a resident crying. Mrs. Smith rushes to her and puts her arm around her. The poor girl sobs in her embrace. Mrs. Smith asks me with her eyes. "Another time?"

I nod quietly and back out. In the elevator, the song "Happy" starts to play again in my mind, but the dance routine is replaced by a Golden God with an emerald green gaze, smiling at me.

Walking down the hall to my apartment, I decide not to text Cat about my return after all.

Once inside, I get a beer from the refrigerator and take it onto the balcony. I sip it slowly, enjoying the cold brew on this mild day. *I have some thinking to do. My life just changed in the span of an hour. I sure didn't see this in my stars.*

CHAPTER TWO

I wake up to the sound of birds chirping and my coffee perking. I roll over and bury my head under my pillow. *Gawd, I've learned to hate Mondays!* My body clock refuses to adjust. *It's not natural to rise this early!* I take a deep breath, come out from under the pillow and roll on my back to do my stretches. *Why did I take this job again? Oh yeah, because my Mama needed me here, but didn't actually* need *me and I got bored in this fucked up, hellhole. Stop whining! This is your last week at work and it served your purpose. It filled your time.* As I stretch my legs wide and lean my body over each one touching my face to my skin, kissing my beloved dancing legs, I think back to the day I got the news about her car wreck.

When I missed Daddy's call, he called Cat. She came straight down, let herself in and stood on the edge of my pool. I was swimming laps and didn't see her until she stuck her foot in the water. That scared me bad enough, but when I saw the expression on her face, that scared the shit out of me. She told me what my dad had said. "There weren't any details, but it was a bad wreck and she was hurt." I flew home on

Bart's private jet within an hour of the news and walked in the hospital 7 hours later to find my Daddy sitting all alone in the waiting room with his face in his hands. He explained that she had a severely broken leg and she was in surgery.

I stretch further into a straddle split and roll down to touch my face on the bed.

The next morning when she opened her eyes, she was so happy to see me there. I decided to take a break from my life in Vegas to spend some quality time with them. That was eight weeks ago. Full recovery accomplished and quality time accomplished. So much so, they left me this weekend for a summer sailing vacation around the Virgin Islands! *I love my independent parents!*

Turning my body into a front split, I arch back, bend my knee, grab my foot and pull it to my face. I plant a loud kiss on it, then transition to a straddle split, and repeat on the other leg. Next, I crawl to the edge of the bed where I put my hands on the floor and drag my legs up into a hand stand. I walk to the wall where I do 15 hand stand push-ups. The coffee pot finishes perking on the last one.

Standing and grabbing my iPhone off the night stand, I head for the kitchen to pour myself a strong cup of joe. There is a text from Mama. *Arrived safe.

Excited. Boarding the boat. Will check in soon. Don't worry. Be safe. Love you, pumpkin!*

Smiling, I think of the love my parents have for each other after all these years and the fun they have shared. I've always wanted that for myself and have refused to compromise. "I'm not going to fuck for the sake of fucking." I've told my close friends, who were concerned about my love life. *Love life, the irony of it!* And in Vegas, I explain. "I'm around sex all the time! I don't feel the need to fuck for the sake of fucking." Which some of the girls get, but none of the guys I tried to date in the beginning did. They called me all sorts of names, Ice Queen, Frozen Bitch, Frigid Witch, Hypocrite, Tease, *Whatever.*

Pouring myself a mug, I see Mr. Moore's dark golden hair and his incredible eyes that pierced my core. *He is a fucking fine feast for sure! With superb seduction skills.* Walking out onto the balcony, I hover over the rim, sipping the black liquid. *I can't get over how he turned me on! The chemical connection is surprising. That's never happened to me before! Never! Ever!* I lean on the rail, not really hearing the sounds of the morning. *Maybe my hiatus from all the sex in Vegas has made this an opportune time for my juices to flow and my own desires to rise to the surface. Maybe there could be more with Moore. I like that thought.*

31

Walking back in, I stop at my stripper pole. *I need to work you this evening.*

In the shower, I constantly have to push *him* out of my mind. Rubbing the soap on my body makes *him* keep showing up. Drying off with the towel, I reach this conclusion for sure: *My return to Vegas is on hold in-def.*

At work, the six phone lines for the company that hired me as a short term temp are busy and leave very little time for daydreaming and further contemplation of Mr. Moore. The two men in the front office who work with me, Charlie and TD, are away on business, which is a relief. I can concentrate on my job without having to fend off their flirtatious innuendos and ignore their developing sex triangle.

If they only knew what I really do. I laugh and shake my head. *I'm glad they don't! But if they did, I could make that threesome awesome. There's a lot to work with. Maybe I'll write them a note when I leave and slip it under Charlie's door. A goodbye gift.... Maybe not.*

During lunch, I eat my spoon of peanut butter and let my thoughts turn to Moore. I know nothing about him except that *he is golden and gorgeous, and one hell of a seduction artist. He has refined skills in the subtle art of seduction. His facial expressions. "Ladies first," and "My Lady." His touch when he took my hand. The strokes of his thumbs. All well-developed skills, but it's more than that. It's Moore! Damn, I'm getting hot just thinking about him again.* I pick up my apple and bite into it. *His 'art' reminds me of that Italian tennis star who came to Vegas before I stopped dating. After an enjoyable evening out, in which he exhibited excellent, highly skilled seduction techniques with just the right amount of flirting and flattery, he didn't make it to second base with me. He was very hurt and upset. He, of course, expected a good fuck for his time and money, so my name was trashed in the club the next night. I sent Lei to console him, unbeknownst to him of course, and he soon forgot me. Lei is a pro!*

I open a yogurt. *But Moore is different. His seduction skills are excellent and refined, but it is him. The way his eyes look at me, I can't pull mine away.* I pop a few blueberries in my mouth and chew them letting yesterday replay in my mind. *The first time in the elevator when his gaze pierced my core, that wasn't chemistry. That was something else.* I sip my carrot juice, then throw my lunch away and wipe down the break room table. *All I really know for sure is that he is a stranger that I am extremely attracted to, for once in my life. That's all I know!* I take a deep breath, sigh and walk back to my desk.

Staring out the window, I see a bird flittering around on the sidewalk, then another one joins it. They flirt, then fly off to fuck. I put my face in my hands. *I'm so lonely! How did my life get so complicated?* I put my pencil to my lips, running it back and forth. The feeling makes me think of how the intensity of his look in the elevator made me lick my lips, and I see his grin. I get up and pace the floor. *I need a plan to see him today.*

When 4 o'clock rolls around, I hit the door with a smile. Pulling out of the parking lot, plan in place, butterflies begin to fly around my tummy and I giggle. *He makes me feel alive! And it feels fucking fantastic!*

At Publix, I walk through the doors with purpose and direction. The cashiers all know me and Janice, who is in the express lane again today, pokes fun at me. "Siri, back so soon? Weren't you in here yesterday? Did you forget something?"

I laugh and joke with her. "I'm out of wine and I came in too friggin' early yesterday. I forgot you can't buy alcohol on Sunday until one o'clock. It's like y'all are in the Southern Bible Belt or something so I had to swing by on my way home tonight."

"Yeah! I follow ya! I guess 'Sin City' stays open and turned on 24/7?"

"Yes, it does! You should come out and try it sometime. You might not come home for years either."

"Yeah, right! I'm not going to hell." She blurts out before she realizes she just condemned me. "Sorry. I'll say a prayer for you."

"It's okay, Janice. I'm not offended. And I appreciate the kind thought."

She focuses on my items. "And the cookies? What's up with the junk food? I thought you were a total health food nut."

"Yeah, well. They are for a friend … as a gift." I laugh. "Don't look so shocked! Not everyone has shunned me. I have friends here." After a dramatic pause, I roll my eyes, making her and the bag boy laugh. "Ok. Only one."

Out on the express way, traffic has come to a standstill. *Shit! There must be a wreck. I hope no one is hurt.* As I inch forward, I see the delay. It isn't a wreck. There are cows in the road and Sheriff Deputies are trying to herd them on foot. *That ain't gonna work, boys. You need some cowboys on horses, or we'll have to wait until feeding time when the cows will all go home on their own. I might as well work on "Happy."* I take my iPhone out, play it on repeat, study the choreography and jot notes.

When I enter the parking lot, I'm almost 2 hours later than usual, but I squeal with delight when I see his Raptor. My usual parking spot is taken so I have to drive around to the rear lot. *I should really mention to management that they could charge an optional monthly fee for assigned parking.* I find a spot and wedge in between two minivans. Grabbing the wine and box of cookies, I decide to take a short cut through the running trail and come in the rear. In the elevator, I push #9 and see Mrs. Smith laughing and talking outside the entrance to someone. *She looks like she is flirting. I wonder if she has a love interest. Good for her!*

When I get off the elevator, I turn to look down to his door. *My new neighbor! Woo Hoo!* Once inside my apartment, I set the bottle of wine and cookies down on the counter and rush to my bedroom to strip off the business suit and sports bra I wear to hide my figure. While I sat waiting on the cows, my mind floated back to Moore, and I chose a tangerine color push-up bra with matching tank top, a pair of cream color linen beach pants and flat sandals to wear. Slipping them on, I look in the mirror. *I look casual, comfy and curvy.* Snatching the wine and cookies up, I hit the door.

Standing in the hall outside his apartment, I take several deep breaths to keep the butterflies at bay.

Nervous butterflies? For Zeus sake, why do I have butterflies? I'm fucking Seary! A Vegas star! But I take a couple of additional deep breaths, then raise my knuckles and knock. I wait a minute and then knock again. No answer. *Hmm....* A wave of disappointment falls over me and I turn to head back to my place. *Oh, shit! He was only signing the papers today. Holy Hades!* I take off at a run to my apartment. *He was here when I came home. I bet he was the one flirting with Mrs. Smith! He was waiting on me! And I came in the back!* Once inside, I set the cookies and wine on the counter and rush to my balcony. His truck is leaving the parking lot. The air in my balloon escapes. I feel deflated. I stand there watching his Raptor travel down the drive through the gaps in the trees until it is gone from sight. Plopping onto my lounge chair, I grunt. "Fuck!"

The next morning, I am resolved to find out when his move-in day actually is from Mrs. Smith. *I don't want to experience that kind of disappointment again.* I tossed and turned all night, pissed at myself that I didn't think of the obvious. She doesn't arrive into the office until 9 o'clock and I call at exactly 9 o'clock. "Mrs. Smith, this is Siri Wright in 9A."

"Oh, yes dear, what can I do for you?"

"Listen, I was wondering if you could tell me what day Mr. Moore is moving in? I thought it would be nice to take him a welcome gift."

"Oh, sweetie, that is so thoughtful of you. You know how military men are. They are always being uprooted and all. A welcome gift is such a nice idea. You know I stayed late yesterday talking to him. He was waiting to see you, but he had to leave before you made it home."

"There was a herd of cows on the express lane, and I was stuck in traffic. I hate I missed him."

"He is quite smitten with you, dear. He was trying to get some information on you, but I told him I couldn't divulge anything because of privacy issues."

"What did he want to know?"

"How long you had been here and how long a lease you signed."

"He did? Did he say why he wanted to know?"

"No. You know how pilots are. Well, maybe you don't, but they are very concise communicators. He didn't say why, but he must have a reason for asking. My first husband was a helicopter pilot too." *He's a helicopter pilot! Cool!* "It was very frustrating talking to him. I was always playing 20 questions to pry information out of him. It didn't last. We divorced after…."

I clear my throat.

"Oh dear me, I didn't mean to rattle on. Where was I?"

"You were about to tell me how long a lease he signed."

"Oh, yes. He took the 3 month lease, which I thought was curious."

"Why was that curious?"

"Well, I must have misunderstood, you know I do get confused sometimes, but I could have sworn he told me his buddy coming in for training would need a year lease. Well, anyway, it doesn't matter really."

What? A buddy? What the fuck? NO! I try to keep the panic out of my voice. "Mrs. Smith, now *I'm* confused. Who rented the apartment?"

"Mr. Moore."

"I know Mr. Moore rented it but for whom? His buddy or himself?" I hold my breath, waiting for her answer.

"Well, that was curious too. He put his own name on the lease."

I blurt out. *"Fuck! You had me scared there for a moment."* Then, I quickly blurt an apology. "Oh shit, excuse my language."

She laughs. "My Dear, I'm happy he rented it too. He does seem like such a nice young man and you two would make quite a cute couple!"

"Thanks, Mrs. Smith." I agree with her to keep her talking. "So, do you know what day he is moving in?"

"Oh, yes, your welcome gift. Today."

Today! He is moving in today! YAY! I feel those damn nervous butterflies replace the breath that was held in my gut, but I'm okay with that. *It beats a deflated balloon!*

"Do you know what time?"

"No, only that it is today, but he isn't here yet."

"Thank you, Mrs. Smith."

"You're welcome, hun. We don't do enough for our service men and women."

"No ma'am, we don't."

"You know I met my first husband at the gas station by the post gate. He looked so handsome in his uniform…." She blabs on while I dial our office number from line 6. When it rings, I politely tell her I have to answer that.

The rest of my day is spent answering the phones and doodling little hearts and halo's all over my pad while Mr. Moore's face constantly floats across my mind. At 4 o'clock, I hit the door again, all smiles and butterflies knowing that tonight I will be enjoying Merlot and cookies for supper and *who knows what for dessert.*

When I pull into the parking lot at 4:20, his big 'bad ass' black truck is parked next to my usual space which is empty so I whip right in. *Show time in 15.* Walking in, I glance at the office and Mrs. Smith is standing in the doorway. She smiles and waves, then points upstairs and gives me the ok sign. I smile back and give her the ok sign too. *Nothing like having a spy and good Intel.*

Once in my place, I hum "Happy" while I change into the same tangerine outfit, put the cookies in the oven on low, and tie a blue ribbon around the wine bottle. I find a basket to transport the cookies, put them on a plate, throw a towel over them, grab the bottle of wine and float down to 9G.

At the door, I lift the towel off the cookies and their aroma fills the air. After several deep breaths to calm myself, I raise my knuckles to knock. Mr. Moore pulls the door open, takes a step to come out, then stops surprised to see me. He gives me his big beautiful smile. "Miss Wright, I missed you yesterday."

My butterflies fly away as my tummy lurches so hard I almost pee my pants. *Fucking A! He is hotter than I remember!* The light from the hall shines in his eyes and on his hair. *They really are bright emerald green! And it really does give a halo effect!* My mouth waters.

Managing somehow to keep my composure, I look past him into his apartment and see that it's dark. "Is this a bad time?"

As he studies my outfit, the basket on my arm, and the bottle of wine in my hand, I study his face in greater detail. His dark, almost black, eyebrows accentuate his eyes to perfection. His white teeth stand out against his tanned skin and are perfectly straight. His lips…. *How could I have missed his lips? They are defined, perfectly shaped, but not full, and not tight; they are goldilocks perfect. They are just right.* I lick my own.

He inhales the scent of the cookies. "Of course not. Please come in." He turns the lights back on and pulls the door all the way open, gesturing for me to enter. When I walk in, I pause just inside. "I can always find time for a beautiful woman who comes knocking on my door bearing gifts of cookies and wine." The tone of his deep voice envelopes and caresses my ears. His hands brush my skin and I feel the tingle he gives me as he lifts the basket off my arm and takes the wine out of my hand. As he walks away, I watch his perfect physique. I notice several very nice things. One, he *is* wearing a flight suit. Two that flight suit shows off his perfect v-shaped body.

Three that flight suit shows off his killer, perfect, coffee bean shaped ass too. *A fucking fine feast!* When he is in the kitchen, he motions for me join him. "I'm sorry, but I can't enjoy a glass with you right now of this…" He holds the wine bottle away so he can read the label. "…fine Merlot. I'm flying tonight, but I will definitely give you a raincheck." He sets it on the counter with the basket of cookies. "I will be happy to devour these delicious morsels with you now though. Would you like a glass of milk?"

I laugh to myself. *Men! They are suckers for milk and cookies.* I walk up to the counter watching how comfortable he is in his new apartment. *He has made himself right at home in a matter of hours.* He gestures to one of the bar stools so I sit. He grabs two lowball glasses without waiting for my answer, and the milk from the refrigerator, then pours us both a glass. He stands on the opposite side, takes a cookie, dunks it in his milk, then plops it in his mouth whole. "Yum." He says as he closes his eyes. "Have one. They are delicious."

I stare at his mouth working on the cookie. The motion of his lips pushes an 'on' button I didn't know I had. *Yum, your lips! They form a perfect heart shape.* The thought of sucking his bottom lip fills my mind and I bite my own staring fascinated and captivated. *Deliciousness.* When he swallows, they stop moving, then they begin to part slightly, spreading over his teeth into a 'sexy as hell' smile. I lift my eyes to find him watching me through hooded lids. The desire I see there sends a hot wave coursing through me and I blush, *busted*, but I smile back. *Like minds are a good thing.*

He picks another cookie up. "Here. Like this." His eyes hold mine as he dunks it. Then my eyes fall to his open mouth, as he slowly inserts it between his sexy lips again, but this time, he allows more tongue to greet it. As he lays the cookie on his flat tongue, and slowly draws it into his mouth, another wave of desire crashes over me. My breathing quickens.

Despite the fact that I know he is looking for my reaction, I can't control myself. Watching his lips move as he chews makes me bite my lip again. *Damn, he pushes my 'on' buttons.*

He chuckles as he picks up another cookie and hands it to me. "Your turn. Let me see what you can do with it."

My eyes twinkle at him. *Yes. Let me show you what I can do with a cookie. Let me push your buttons, Mr. Moore.*

Taking the cookie, I hover it over my milk. I wait until his eyes leave mine and travel to the cookie, then I dunk it in my milk, once, twice, three times in a rhythm that matches our thoughts. The milk dances in the glass. His eyes watch its journey to my fully opened mouth. Laying the cookie on my flat tongue, I bare my teeth, biting it gently, then I curl my tongue up between my fingers, and pull the rest of the delicious morsel in. Moaning, I chew and chew and chew, working my mouth around and around. Tipping my head all the way back so my neck is fully extended, I close my eyes and swallow, once, twice, three times. I let my own 'sexy as hell' smile spread slowly over my teeth. "That was delicious!" When I cut my eyes to look at him, his eyes are a dark shade of emerald green. I know what he is thinking *and it isn't how good that damn cookie tastes.*

Picking my head up, I look straight into his eyes, confident I won that round. His eyes bore into mine for several seconds. My confidence turns into something much more primitive as he smiles that sexy half smile again and challenges me. "Oh, no. You can do better than that. No biting."

I raise my eyebrows and smirk. We stare at each other with the innuendo heavy between us. I drop my eyes to stare at my milk, not really seeing it. *Challenge received.* I can feel him watching me, looking for my reaction. *I really want to fuck you,*

Mr. Moore. I twist the glass. *No sense denying that.*
"That's not very lady like."

He smirks at me thinking he has won, that I'm
backing down. Swinging my hair so it is all on one
side, I look up at him from under my lashes.
Challenge accepted. His expression changes. As I
reach for a cookie, hungry eyes wanting me, watch
me. I smirk with confidence as I hover it over my
milk again. *You are never again going to dunk a
cookie without seeing this replayed.* I wait until his
eyes travel to the cookie, then I dunk it in the milk
with such force that it sloshes. Pulling the cookie
back to the edge, I pause, then I dunk it hard again,
sloshing the milk again, then withdraw it to the edge.
His breathing changes. Once more, I slam the cookie
into the milk and it sloshes over the top. I lean up,
push my tits down onto the counter so they pop out
of the neckline of my tank top, pucker my lips, and
suck the milk from the cookie. His breathing stops.
You weren't expecting that. My tongue darts around
my parted lips as I arch my back, thrusting my tits
toward him, until my neck is fully extended and
exposed again. Sticking my tongue out, I insert the
whole cookie into my abyss. Closing my mouth
around my thumb, I suck it, once, twice, three times.
Then I slide it in and out, once, twice, three times. As
I massage the cookie around my mouth, once, twice,

three times, I hear a very low, primal groan from him. Knowing I have won the cookie eating contest, I swallow the whole fucking thing, once! Another low groan escapes him. Laying my head sidewise as I lick my lips, confident I have made him horny as hell, I smirk. "Like that?"

His hooded eyes and his hungry expression were nothing compared to the dark look on his face now. *It looks like a storm! Battle ready.* My body freezes. *I have tested his self-control.* Wide eyed, I watch him struggling, knowing instinctively not to move, to wait. For all my experiences in Vegas, I have never seen this expression before. The intensity is truly as frightening as it is exciting. I can see and feel the ferocity of his passion. It looks and feels like a storm. *Holy fucking hell!* The electricity between us sends my hand to reach for him and his eyes dart to it, then they look directly into mine. The piercing power touches something deep inside me and whatever it is comes alive! My tits swell and the nipples shrink, elongate and push out on my bra. My pussy soaks my pants and my clit tingles. *Damn, that look turns me on! He is a fucking fine Beast who would feast on me!* I pull my hand back. *I would let you fuck me right now, Mr. Moore, and that's never happened to me before!*

"Damn straight. Just like that." He growls. As we stare at each other, I wonder. *How? How can this happen between us so fast?* He closes his eyes, hangs his head, and leans on the counter. I can see his tense, bulging muscles under his taut flight suit. I watch him controlling himself with his breath. Slowly, his expression subsides and his muscles relax. He shakes his hanging head. When he lifts his face to mine again, he is grinning. "Damn, woman." The corners of his eyes crinkle a tiny bit.

He's just too damn cute! My heart starts to sing. Grinning back at him, the mischievous twinkle appears in my eyes and I reach for a cookie. His eyes flare slightly and I see a trace of concern flash across his face. I smile sweetly at him. *Don't worry. I'm not going to push your buttons again. Not yet, anyway.* I hold the cookie out to him. "Yum. Have one. I hear they are delicious." He chuckles as he takes the cookie. I giggle. "They are to die for!"

He dunks it. "Are you from around here?" He stuffs his gorgeous face as he waits for my answer, relaxed and comfortable again.

"Yes and no. I'm complicated."

"No doubt." He rolls his eyes, making me laugh.

"And you? Are you from around here?"

"Yes and no too. I'm complicated too." He flirts, mimicking me.

"No doubt." I roll my eyes, mimicking him with a teasing tone.

We each take another cookie, grinning at each other. "So, what are you doing this weekend?" He stuffs his mouth.

"Nothing." I nibble mine. "Why?" My eyes dance.

He watches my mouth on my cookie as he chews. "Oh, I was just wondering what exactly goes on around here on the weekends."

"Not a whole helluva lot. You have to make your own entertainment."

His eyes light up. "What kind of entertainment do you make?"

"Personally, I entertain myself with exercise." I finish my cookie. "I'm turning into an exercise freak."

"An exercise freak? Really?" He asks, keeping a straight face, but his eyes are dancing. "What kind of exercise?"

"Dancer-cise. I'm actually a dancer in my complicated life." I reach for another cookie.

"I know. I've been dreaming about you ever since I saw you dance."

"I'm surprised you could tell I was a dancer." I plop the cookie in my mouth whole and look up as I push the basket to him, waving that I'm finished.

"Well, I …" He stares at the basket, thinking. "Yes. Well…" He puts his hand on the basket. "I've been replaying your dance moves over and over in my mind." He looks at me and smiles.

"In that first five minutes Sunday?" I grin up at him, disbelief on my face.

He watches me for a moment, then pulls the basket to him and takes the last two cookies. "There was a very dramatic dance move in that 5 minutes."

I laugh. "Now that was an unforgettable performance!"

"Yes, parts of it certainly were." He plops both cookies in his mouth.

I talk with my hands. "Let me guess, it was the impressive jump with the twirling spin I performed perfectly to avoid the collision?"

He laughs and shakes his head. "No, actually it was the way you flipped your hair, dropped your ass and … the way certain parts bounced that stuck with me." He stares at my tits. "Pretty amazing move." He looks into my face and smiles. "You are unforgettable."

I tingle from his look and his words. Dropping my eyes, I grin at my milk and twist my glass again. "Umm hmm."

"Back to your weekend plans, I was hoping we could share the wine one day, if you aren't busy."

"That would be nice. I would like that."

"But right now, I have to run. I don't want to be late." He commands. "Finish your milk."

I obediently pick my glass up to drain it, but decide to make a toast first. I hold the glass up for him to clink. "Here's to … Moore."

He holds his up. "Here's to … Wright." We touch glasses then drain them. He washes them quickly and wipes off the counter.

I watch this gorgeous specimen in action. *His fluid motion and efficient movement is sexy as hell! Is there nothing that isn't perfect?*

He hands me my basket. "I really hate to eat and run."

I finish his sentence as he follows me to the door. "But duty calls?"

"Something like that." He locks the door behind us.

As we walk down to the elevator, he asks. "So where's the 'no' you are from?" I tip my head not understanding his question. "Where does the complicated dancer live?"

I smile looking at the floor. We walk a few steps before I answer. "Vegas." I cut my eyes to see his reaction.

"Awesome. Vegas is one of my favorite places in the world."

"I don't usually tell folks from here that. Not because I'm ashamed, because I'm not. I love my life! But because they can't handle it. You know, Sin City. To them, Vegas is the capital of Hell." I laugh, thinking of Janice's comments at the Publix checkout line. "And I'm going straight there." I shake my head and look at him. "It's really rather sad to me. I pity them as much as they pray for me. I'm the one who doesn't judge others. I'm the one who actually loves everyone, no matter who they are, or where they come from. I'm the one who values honesty above lies."

He half turns, and gives me an impressed look. "You are really an interesting find."

I smirk and half turn to him too. "Now how sad is that? Honesty is interesting. No, even worse, honesty is a find?" I bump into him playfully as we walk. "So, where is the 'no' you are from?"

"Army brat and Army helicopter pilot. I have family in Italy too, and bounce back and forth from here to there, but I lived here the longest so I call it home."

Italian! I knew it! "I've always wanted to go to Italy, particularly Florence and Rome. I love architecture and the arts." I say as we reach the elevator. "Thank you for your service too. Did you serve in Afghanistan or Iraq?"

He gives me a quick nod of acknowledgement as he pushes the down button. "Both." Then he invades my personal space and speaks quietly to me. "Thanks for the cookies."

My body is instantly turned on and wanting his touch. I answer as quietly looking into his gorgeous face. "You're welcome."

"I enjoyed watching you enjoy them."

My eyes twinkle. "I enjoyed watching you … enjoy watching me … enjoy them."

His eyes twinkle with mine. "Did you bake them yourself?"

"Ha, no! I can't cook." I confess. "Compliments of the bakery in Publix."

"Your honesty is refreshing, you know."

"So I've been told."

The elevator arrives and he says in my ear. "I'll be dreaming of the way you eat cookies for the rest of my life." My ear tingles from his tone all the way down to my toes and I close my eyes enjoying the sensation. "And I can't wait to see what you will do with wine." I feel him back away. I open my eyes to see him in the elevator, pushing the lobby button. As the doors close, he says. "You are more than I dreamed of." His smile is so beautiful that my knees get weak. He says in the last shrinking span. "Ciao."

"See ya." When the doors are closed, I run to my apartment, fling the basket on the counter, and rush out onto the balcony. Bracing on the rail, I lean over it. As soon as he exits the building, he turns to look to my apartment. I wave and he throws his hand up, then walks with his perfect posture and strong gait to his truck. He gives me another wave as he gets in. I wave again too. As his truck backs out, I hug myself. *I want Moore!* As I watch his truck disappear down the private drive to the highway, I sing one of my favorite runway dance songs. "So Contagious" by Acceptance. *Def! Unexpected!*

Standing in the evening air, I know he has stirred something inside me, and I will never be the same.

CHAPTER THREE

Wednesday morning, I roll over and stare at the dark ceiling. I put my pillow over my face. *Siri! For Zeus sake, the sun isn't even up yet. Why are you awake?* I pull the pillow off. *Because my dreams were full of Moore with me in Vegas.* Putting the pillow under my head, I lay there enjoying those visions, but they soon start to fade. *Why is it when you wake, you lose your dreams? Now all I can remember is that I kept seeing Moore's face scattered in the crowd. And I was unbelievably happy.* Closing my eyes, I doze off with a content smile on my face.

As soon as the sun breaks the sky, I do my stretches with my mind full of Moore and the possibilities of him in Vegas. I see him in my pool, swimming laps, naked. I see him on my balcony sunning, naked, with me. I see him in my bed, naked, on top of me. *Yum.* Flipping on my stomach, I drag myself to the edge of the bed and repeat my handstand ritual. *I really need to work my pole tonight. I've been neglecting it.*

In the kitchen, I wait for the coffee to finish perking. My Blue Heart souvenir mug is sitting next to it. Smiling, I pick it up to admire the autograph.

Surreal's name in her flowery handwriting, complete with a heart on the S, is in blue matching ink. It brightens my mood even more. *I'm so fortunate!* Pouring my coffee, I take it out onto the balcony.

This time of year the Dogwood trees and Azalea bushes are in full bloom. *It is exquisite.* Blowing on my coffee then taking a long sip, I think about last night. *Moore is obviously as attracted to me as I am to him ... which is pretty damn attracted. Damn, that dark look on his face. That expression! Wow! I was so turned on!* My pussy tightens at the memory of it. *I wonder what day he wants to have wine. Not that it matters, I'm free anytime. I'll need to think of something super sexy to do with it. I could do a handstand, pick it up off the table with my legs and walk it to him. Or I could cup his wine glass in my ass, or even better, my tits, then pour it into his open mouth. Or, I could push my tits together making a cleavage vessel and he could drink from them. Or, I could pour it down his body and lick it off him.* I take a deep breath and sigh. *I've waited so long to meet someone. I'm ready for some fucking fireworks!* I take another long sip of coffee. *And when he said I'm more than he dreamed of, my knees got weak.*

I walk to the side rail of the balcony and stare at the jogging trail without seeing it. *I wonder if he meant he had actually dreamt of me, or if he meant I was more than the ideal girl he dreams about. Fuck, Siri! What difference does it make? They were beautiful words.*

What will I do today to see him before he leaves to fly? I focus my eyes on the runners jogging off the trail. *That's easy. I'll run after work. Perfect! Now, which trail? Oh, Holy Hades, there he is. Damn, he is beautiful.* The sun is glistening off his golden halo and the sweat on his body. He is wearing only a pair of red running shorts. *He's hot as Hades!* His pecs are bouncing gently with each jog. When he hits the sidewalk, he walks around for his cool down. *WOW!* The dramatic distance between his broad shoulders and his small waist can be seen even this far away. *He looks like a body builder! I wonder if he competes.*

He glances up to my balcony and seeing me, throws his hand up. I let go of the grip that seized my mug and wave back, but now he isn't looking at me. A couple of girls jogging by have stopped to chat him up. I see them pointing out the laundry mat and the club house. *They are obviously making sure he knows where to find them.* He excuses himself, walks a couple of steps then looks up to the balcony at me again. I wave again and this time he sees me. He waves, then continues walking to the building. The girls, who watched his ass as he walked off, look up to see me too. *That's right, bitches.* I smile down on them, turn and go back inside.

I think about opening my door so I can see him when he gets off the elevator, but I think better about it. *That would only lead to Moore immediately. Go get a cold shower and get to work. You can dream about him all day and 'bump' into him tonight.*

This day at work is a repeat of yesterday's doodles. I find out that Charlie and TD will be back tomorrow so I have plenty of time to think about Moore, the golden man in 9G. *He's just too damn cute! His eyes and hair when he opened the door! The way his flight suit laid on top of his ass leaving nothing to my imagination. I've seen way too many asses not to know that's a perfect fucking muscle.* I replay the cookie eating challenge. His dark expression, then the frightening one. *I'd love to know what is going through his mind when that look is on his face! Maybe I'll find out!* I smirk to myself. I replay the conversation we had when we were walking down the hallway, over and over. *We interact really well with each other. His comments about me being an interesting find, honesty being refreshing and more than he dreamed of are at the top of the best comments ever list.* The view of his body this morning, all hot and sweaty even 9 stories away, leaves me day dreaming about what the weekend will bring.

The day passes without anything eventful happening. I take the time to write the suggestion about the assigned parking spots. I add a special request for coming up with the idea: that I be given my usual spot and Moore be given the one next to me. *Mrs. Smith will arrange it for me.*

When 4 o'clock comes, I'm gone. Skillfully maneuvering my car into the parking spot next to his, I drop the suggestion in the suggestion box outside the office door and hurry to my apartment. I get a water from the refrigerator to hydrate as I change into my running clothes. I've already decided on what I will wear. I have a pale yellow, low cut sports bra that keeps everything from bouncing but shows cleavage, covered by an oversized, white cropped tank top that doesn't hide anything, and accentuates the size of my tits, and short, black jogging shorts.

Walking to the elevator, I keep my eyes fixed on 9G. If he came out now, it would be even better, but he doesn't. No one is in the elevator and no one stops it so I have a quiet ride down. Once outside, I stretch on the sidewalk, then hit the trail starting slow, warming up then burning the pace. Sprinting to the finish, breathing hard, with a good sweat running down my back. I finish and cool down exactly as planned. I'm pacing up and down the area outside the lobby watching for the elevator doors to open. When they do and I see Moore inside, I casually enter the lobby.

Moore emerges right on cue and our eyes lock immediately. My tummy lurches hard, doing the familiar back flip as we walk to each other. *He looks good! But he's not in his flight suit.* He is wearing a plain, white t-shirt that lies softly on those muscular pecs with his name stenciled across the front, with a pair of light weight, navy blue, soft shorts and white converse tennis shoes. The white color makes his dark skin look healthy and radiant, matching his smile, which he freely gives me. *Will I ever get used to the shock of how fucking cute he is? I hope not!* Watching him walk to me makes me tingle. *There is something special about the way he carries himself. I can't quite put my finger on it. Perfect posture. Obviously an athlete. He's confident, but not cocky. There's something else about the way he carries himself that makes him stand apart from the other guys. He glides gracefully and smooth, but it's not like a cat. There is an air of something else.* I'm momentarily at a loss for words. As he draws closer, his smile is now the same relaxed smile he gave me the first time I laid eyes on him. That smile sends the words to my lips as a vision of him close up without a shirt and without shorts floats by. I whisper to myself. "Like a God! He walks like a God." I laugh, first impressions are usually right. *He is a Golden God!*

"Hi." He says when he draws even, stopping to talk.

"Hi. Looks like you are heading out."

"That's affirmative." His phone goes off. "I have a friendly game of basketball with the bros on post." He hits ignore. "I've gotta run." But he doesn't move. His eyes travel up and down my body. "Looks like you had a good run. You look hot."

That feels more like a compliment than a statement. My tingling gets stronger. "Yep."

"You are in great shape." His eyes run up and down me again, making me get even hotter. "And I bet you have great stamina being both a dancer and an exercise freak." His eyes crinkle.

"Yep." I smile. "I run at a pretty good clip for a girl too." I punch his arm playfully. His muscles are firm and thick. "I bet you couldn't run off and leave me."

His face gets serious. His eyes take and hold mine. My mouth waters with his look. "I would never run off and leave you." He shakes his head. *Are we talking about running now or something more?* "If you decide to … run with me, I promise to hang around." His face looks so sincere. *Oh man, your eyes are touching my heart. That's definitely more.*

Two guys with military haircuts, dressed like him, come in.

He gives me a sheepish smile. "My basketball bros."

I laugh. "Obviously."

"Moore. Bro! Come on." One of them calls to him.

Moore waves them off. "Would you like to come watch?"

"Oh, hell no! No bitches allowed. It's the only night I can get away from mine. Excuse me, ma'am. Nothing personal."

"It's all good. I can't tonight anyway." As I turn to walk away, Moore reaches out, stopping me. My skin sings.

The married bro hangs his head. "Shit. She wins. We might as well go wait in the car."

The other one calls over his shoulder as he is led out by the married dude. "Just because you resigned, doesn't mean you aren't obligated anymore!"

I laugh at them. Moore strokes my arm with his thumb and goosebumps pop out. I look back at him. His eyes are asking me to come, but I tell him. "I'll take a raincheck."

"That's two, right? The first one is the bottle of wine and now this one."

"Yes. Two." He lets my arm go and I walk to the elevator.

He stands there watching me. I hit the up button. "Hey Wright,"

I turn back to look at him. "Yes Moore?"

"That's an awesome ride you drive."

My eyes twinkle. "I'll take you for a wild ride sometime."

"I bet you will … Wild Thang."

I laugh at that. "Your ride is pretty spectacular too."

"Yes, I'll give you the ride of your life."

"I'll hold you to that." The elevator doors open. I back in and hit #9. "See ya!" Our eyes lock as the doors close. My world shrinks to his piercing eyes.

"Ciao."

When he is gone, I lean on the back wall rolling my eyes, and holding my heart. "This is crazy! I've got to text Cat and tell her everything."

In my apartment, I head first for the shower. While the water washes away my sweat, I sing "Halo" with Angie Miller at the top of my lungs, sticking my head in and out of the water.

I know I built walls, but they tumbled down, without any objection, that instant we saw each other.

The instant I saw his halo. Did I find an angel? No, I found a God. A Golden God! I feel so alive! My heart has awakened. I know he is a risk. That I don't know him, but he's worth it. I can't shut him out! I just can't! I see him every moment now. He consumes my mind! He has the power to save me. He is perfect! Everything I ever said I wanted in a man. I feel his halo. He is a Golden God. I see on his face, he feels it too! We have something special between us.

I can explain what happened in the elevator now. That first piercing moment. He pierced me like a ray of sun in the darkness. No, like a lightning bolt in a storm! No! Not a lightning bolt! Like a thunder clap! Yes! Like thunder! Oh, his darkness rolls like thunder!

I can't believe this is happening. I've never fallen for anyone before like this. It just feels ... right! I laugh. I see him saying, "Wright" and I hear myself saying, "Moore" and I know he gets our word play on our names. I'm his Miss Wright and he is who I want Moore of! *I'm flying so high, gravity has nothing on me! I feel fucking fantastic! I see his halo. I feel his smile as it lands on my face. OH! This feels so right! He is all I need. Don't fade away! I have to see him again, and again, and again!*

I look up to the heavens as I turn the water off. "I don't want this feeling or this man to ever fade away. Let's be clear on that."

Putting the towel around me, I pat myself down, step out, then hang it over the towel rack on the wall to dry. When I turn around, I see myself in my full length mirror behind the door. Standing naked, I examine my body for the one millionth time. It's a regular part of being a dancer and performer. I hear Cat's voice as she tells us. "It's your money maker. You have to examine it regularly." She tells all her new recruits during training. "Your body is a gold mine. Cash in on it while you are in your prime. There will be time later for using your brains to make money. Work your God given assets. Be fruitful! We are Eve's children. Go out and act like her! Seduce!" The Eve reference always makes me laugh being from the Deep South, but it also gets me pumped and ready for action.

I stare at my reflection. I'm petite, and while that's unacceptable in most modeling circles, it is perfect for the entertainment role I have. Cat told me. "It's easy to make yourself appear taller or heavier, but it's next to impossible to make yourself appear shorter and thinner. We can make you anyone you want to be with the right makeup, wig and props, but *you* have to make everyone believe it."

I stretch my arms over my head and give my tits a self-examination. *Beautiful boobs.* I see my grandmothers face when she saw me the summer my tits popped out. *Well dear, you can strike ballerina off your list of dance careers.* I cup my DD's and jiggle them.

I asked Cat during my training. "But what about my big boobs? How do you make them appear smaller?"

"Don't be silly! Everyone wants beautiful tits like yours. They stay real."

I tell my reflection. "The natural movement is something money can't buy and always, always draws the attention of a man's eye."

I flex my tummy. It's tight and flat, but not ripped. "Men don't want to see a hard, lean body builder on a pole. They want to see a curvy dancer, who has a strong and extremely flexible body." *I am stacked and packed!* I flex my biceps and kiss my guns.

Spinning around to view my ass, I cup my cheeks like I did my boobs and jiggle them. *My ass is booty-ful and bountiful.*

Facing the mirror again, I frame my Lovers Heart with my thumbs and fingers, saluting myself. It's my own personal trade mark. When I had my pubic hair removed by laser, I decided to leave a small patch shaped like a heart on the mound. It isn't very big and I keep it buzzed short. It is about an inch in diameter, but it symbolizes so much for me. The bottom point ends where my pussy begins. Hunching my hips, I apply a little blue hair mascara just for myself. Turning to exit, I blow myself a kiss. *I like my looks. I don't think I would change anything.*

Walking into my bedroom, I pick up my iPhone, plop on my bed and text Cat. *Hey, Lady. Met a guy. A fucking fine feast! Can't breathe around him.* I hit send and wait.

She doesn't respond immediately so I roll on my back, stretch my arms over my head and wait. *She is probably at the bar checking the liqueur levels about now. Then she'll do a quick head count backstage to see which dancers are there warming up. She'll check her text in-between to see if anyone is calling in sick.* I sigh. *I miss that lifestyle but it's been good to get away and really rest. I feel rejuvenated. Fresh. As my granddaddy would have said, 'Rip roaring, ready to go!'*

I envision Cat walking in the dressing room with her dominatrix outfit on, leaving no doubt to anyone who is in control. She has taught me everything I know, and she still has a lot to teach me. Cat is my teacher, my personal trainer, my mentor, my manager, but most of all, she is my best friend. At somewhere between 35 and 45, she is still one hell of a beautiful woman, one hell of an erotic dancer, and one hell of a pole dancer. No one knows for sure what her age is, but every new recruit asks and then tries to guess. Especially after she dismounts the stripper pole in a demonstration of what she is looking for, or what she expects from them. When the inevitable question is asked, she tells them she is 21, then she explains. "I set fire to my birth certificate in a satanic ritual on my 21st birthday. I will never age." The smart girls always guess 21 after that. *I did.*

My iPhone rings. "Brick House" by the Commodores plays. It's Cat. *Hey baby girl! You've met a man?*

OMG! Yes! He is absolutely gorgeous! I'm so excited

That's dope! How?

He moved into my apartment building.

Sweet! And convenient! :-) What does he do?

Army helicopter pilot.

That's so fly! :) Have you hooked up yet?

No. I don't even know his first name but his last name is Moore.

I can tell you want Moore. ;D

Oh yeah! I'm dreaming of more with Moore.

Hey I have to run. Call me with details.

Ok. I miss you! Give the girls my love and Bart too.

I will. Laters. And she's gone.

I should really try to snap a pic of Moore to send to her. Maybe this weekend over wine. No, before wine, when we still have our clothes on. I smile at the naughty thoughts of how we will drink the merlot. *I better get off this bed before I satisfy myself. I want to be horny, and ready for his fireworks!*

Walking to the living room, I mount the pole and give myself a good physical workout. The rest of the night I spend working on the moves to the "Happy" video and taking notes. I leave my doors open on the balcony so I can listen for Moore's truck, but he doesn't come home before I go to bed.

Laying there, resting, I think about how lucky I am. My job at Been Jammin' in Vegas is actually two fold. First, I perform as an erotic entertainer on the dance floor, free styling and in groups with the other girls, along with the stripper poles and private lap dances under my show name, Seary. It's pronounced the same, but has fire connotations that I love!

And, second, I am Surreal. An anonymous dancer who impersonates celebrities dancing their video's live on our stage or on the dance floor with the crowd. The idea was a complete accident but has propelled me to stardom and riches beyond my wildest dreams. Thanks to the celebrities that bought into the idea, and the choreographers who signed off on it and who sometimes assist with the details, we keep the crowd guessing who is actually performing for them that night. Is it the real celebrity or Surreal?

Jennifer Lopez was the first to participate. *"Let's get the house going!" And she rocked the party! I'll never forget after my costume was on, how nervous I was peeking out to watch her from behind the curtain of the stage, waiting to go on. Damn, she can dance. And the crowd ate it up! They loved having her party with them. When she ran up onto the stage, threw them a kiss and exited into the wing, they chanted her name. When I switched places with her and danced her video for them, they went wild! No one caught on! She pranced out on stage when it was over and the two of us stood side by side looking like twins. A hush fell on the place until she took my hand and held it up. "Let's give it up for Surreal!" The crowd screamed! It was fucking awesome! I'll never forget it!*

Britney Spears was the second celebrity to buy into it. *She came by within the first month too. She was so professional. She wanted to review my performance first. I danced and she gave me her dainty hand clap, then left. She is one of my favorites to dance because everyone knows her work.*

Pretty soon there was, and continues to be, celebrities constantly stopping in for a flash dance. *I've been fortunate enough to work with the likes of Beyoncé, Miley, and Katy Perry, who is also a favorite. Her videos are so elaborate. They are a lot of fun!* I hug myself. *Now, when I take the stage, the whole crowd is guessing if it's the real deal or Surreal. I love my job! And I am fucking killer at it!*

Rolling over to check the time, I wonder if the Golden God's Raptor is back. I get a drink of water and walk onto the balcony. His spot next to my Shelby is still empty. *I'm not sleepy. The night air is pleasant. The moon is up. I'll sit here a little while. Maybe I can catch a glimpse of him walking like a fucking God from his truck to the building. I've got it bad for him!*

While I sit on the lounge chair, my thoughts drift back to the night I was "discovered." It was the summer I graduated from FSU. My college roomie, Piper, and I went to Vegas to celebrate. *We were only supposed to stay a couple of weeks, but when we both got jobs at Coyote Ugly, we thought, 'Hell yeah! Let's stay all summer.' We blew off a lot of steam!* I smile thinking how hard we laughed about how we spent all that good money getting a fine education only to work at a Tits and Ass establishment dancing on the bar and serving people food and drinks. *Living the dream, completely happy!*

But then in September, Piper went home to London. I tried to talk her into staying, but she said she was ready to return to the real world. *"I miss me Mum, Siri, and the rain! It never rains here!"* Not me, I couldn't bring myself to come back to Alabama. I wasn't ready to surrender my youth to the rednecks and hicks from the sticks.

On her way to the airport, Piper stopped by work for one last hug. I held her tight in the parking lot. "I don't know if I will ever see you again." We cried in each other's arms. When the taxi took her out of sight, I was heartbroken, crying my eyes out. *She was the sister I never had.*

Bart was my first customer that day. I introduced myself in a mono-tone. "Hello, my name is Siri. I'll be your waitress today."

"Hello, Siri. I'm Bart." He held out his hand for me to shake.

I took it and looked into his eyes and said in robot like fashion. "Nice to meet you, Bart. Do you know what you want to drink?"

"Your eyes."

"Pardon me?"

"I want to drink in your eyes, Siri. Your eyes are practically glowing. Did you know that?"

"Oh, yes, sorry. They do that when I cry."

"I'm not sorry I've seen your green eyes glowing. They are crucial!"

"Thank you, Bart. That's awfully nice of you to say."

"Why were you crying?" I tell him the quick version of the whole sob story. "It'll be ok." He told me, and it was. His next questions were about dancing. "I've seen you dancing on the bar. You're very good."

"Thanks."

"No. I sincerely mean that. You are *very* good. Too good to be dancing here. Have you ever thought about dancing in a big club? You could make a lot of money."

"No. Not really. I've been happy here. This is a big bar. But I am going to have to do something to make more money. I can't make ends meet working here without a roomie to share the expenses. What kind of dancing are you talking about? And what kind of money?"

"I've got an idea. Why don't you come tonight to my club and see for yourself. If you're interested in the type of dancing there, we will train you, and in a couple of weeks you can be earning more in tips in a single night than you make all week in here. Would you like that?"

"Maybe. What's the name of your club?" He pulled out his business card and handed it to me. When I read Been Jammin', my mouth fell open. This guy was the owner of the hottest night club in Vegas. Piper and I could never get in.

I decided right then and there that I didn't want to spend that first night without Piper alone, so I took him up on his offer. He sent a limousine to pick me up. When I arrived, the bouncers cleared a path for me and the doorman whisked me in like I was someone important. The place was starting to get cranked up. Bart himself, gave me a quick tour and a quick peek inside a couple of VIP private party rooms. I was surprised to learn that he owns and operates several different businesses under one roof. There is an upscale gentleman's club, along with a fantastic steakhouse, plus the hottest night club in Vegas. It has it all! I was very impressed.

After the tour, he sat me at one of Been Jammin's bars. It has a stage with finger runways that feed several elevated stripper poles, and a big dance floor. He introduced me to the bartender, Cat, and told her to watch over me. He would come get me and have the limo take me home before dawn.

Cat and I hit it off right away. I spent the whole night on that bar stool pouring my heart out to her or on the dance floor dancing the night away. I told her about growing up in rural, south Alabama. How I never fit in with the rednecks and hicks. How I loved men, had a lot of boy friends, but never anyone serious enough to call a boyfriend. How I had never found a man who rocked my world and who I would be willing to follow to the ends of the earth. How I was holding out for that one special guy and refused stubbornly to give up on him. "I know he is out there! It's just a matter of finding him!" I told her how Piper, my English friend who left Vegas today, told me I seriously needed to see a therapist or something. We laughed at that. Cat told me not to give up. I would know him when he walked into my life. 'In the meantime, live it up!'

I now know that Bart was in Coyote Ugly recruiting new talent and thought I had amazing raw skills, so he brought me in for Cat to evaluate. I danced that night but I was only a girl having a night out on the town until Beyoncé's "Dance For You" started to play. When I heard the opening notes, I knew what it was. The choreography of Sheryl Murakami on that video is superb. I could see Beyoncé standing in the door in a raincoat. I couldn't control the dancer within me. She came out.

From my bar stool, I became Beyoncé, dancing exactly like the video. The people closest to me noticed first, then there was a hush that spread like a wave over the room. The only sound was the music. The only one dancing was me. When Beyoncé walks to her man at the desk, I left the bar stool and walked onto the dance floor. The crowd parted, someone produced a chair for me and I danced the whole song right there as Beyoncé, exactly like the video.

When the music stopped, I got a round of applause. I was embarrassed. "Fuck! What have I just done?!" I hid my face and tried to walk back to the barstool, but the crowd closed in. People started pushing each other and trying to touch me. It was crazy! I couldn't see for the phone camera's flashing in my eyes. I was almost in a panic when the crowd parted and Brutus found me. *Sweet, big man, Brutus!* He didn't say a word to me, he escorted me back to my stool with Cat, then took up post behind me. He became my personal body guard that night. *He's had my back ever since. I miss you, you big ole baby!*

Brutus was silent as stone as he posted guard. The people closest were asking him. "Hey man, is that really Beyoncé? Can we get a selfie?" Cat told me she had never seen anything like this before. "People think you *are* Beyoncé. I heard the rumor circulate while you danced." She puts her hand to her ear pretending to be on a phone call. "It's Beyoncé! She's here in the club dancing! Yeah, right now! I'm watching her!"

It was both funny and ridiculous to me, but Cat didn't laugh. She recognized that there was a real gold mine sitting on the bar stool across from her.

The bar did bumper business after the dance. People were pushing their way up to get a selfie snapped with me in the back ground. All I had to do was keep my face turned away. I had curled my hair that night so they saw what they wanted to see. Beyoncé.

Around 4 am, Bart came to get me, he put his arm around me, and whispered in my ear. "Beware, fame is addicting." Then he addressed me in a voice loud enough for the surrounding crowd to hear. "Brutus will take you to your dressing room now. We really appreciate you stopping by and gracing us with your presence."

When I stood up, I kept my clutch in front of my face, blocking all the cameras. The room lit up like the 4th of July. I followed Brutus to the back where he put me in a dressing room and told me. "I'll be right outside the door if you need anything."

"Good Gawd! What happened? This is crazy wild!" I was stunned at the crowd reaction.

Laura was sent in to get me. "You must be Siri. I'm Laura. Those were some pretty impressive dance moves, girl." She had dark brown hair and freckles, but a beautiful slender body with a long waist line and great legs. I liked her from the start. She was a girl just like me; someone who didn't want to go home yet.

"I guess I shouldn't have done it. I got lost in the moment."

"Nonsense! IF you can dance like that, you SHOULD dance like that." She winked. "Besides, it gave me a break. I was on the pole and saw the whole thing. When you flipped your hair the first time, the guys around you turned to watch. When you flipped your hair the second time, everyone around you turned to watch. When you flipped your hair back and spread your legs, the hush started moving through the crowd. By the time you walked around the stool and headed for the dance floor, there wasn't a single person in the room, including me, that wasn't watching Beyoncé. Rumors flew around the whole club that Beyoncé was here dancing."

I stared at her wide eyed. "I knew the room was fooled, but the rumor spread through the whole club? Wow!"

She laughed. "Yes, it did. I'm not shitting you. Bart will be thrilled. You can't buy that kind of publicity!"

Sure enough, the other dancers hurried back to meet Beyoncé, but instead found me. They were all sweet and full of compliments.

When I left that night, Bart 'snuck' me out the back. The paparazzi cameras were flashing. Bart on one side, Cat on the other. We climbed into a limousine and were whisked away. Bart opened a bottle of champagne and toasted me. "Here's to the glowing green eyed vixen who is about to make us all a lot of money."

Seary was hired to dance at his club and the mysterious Surreal was born on September 7 in the back of that limousine. We rode around for a couple of hours brainstorming, hashing out the details, and making sure the paparazzi were gone.

Bart would be my agent. Cat would be my manager. They moved me to the apartment building that Cat owned. She had the penthouse, but I would live in the condo one floor down. *Paradise!*

I trained the next couple of weeks learning to do lap dances, the dance routines with the groups, how to maneuver the stripper pole, and an array of celebrity dance videos while Bart hammered out the details with the singer's agents, the choreographer's and the legal teams. We would pay them a cut of the entire take on the nights when I danced under their name, doing their routine.

Cat was delighted when she discovered that I could dance anyone. "You are a natural talent, baby girl! I'm so happy we found you! What a waste it would have been if you had not been discovered." It has been a win/win for everyone.

I look at my phone, it's well after midnight. *Moore is partying with the bros.* I finally give it up and go to bed.

CHAPTER FOUR

Thursday morning, the sun has to wake me. When I check the time, I freak! *SHIT! I'm going to be late!* I throw on my suit and run to my car. Once in it, I make up time easily. I walk in with a minute to spare, but no one notices. Charlie and TD are not in yet. They arrive mid-morning in golf shirts.

Charlie greets me. "Good morning, Siri."

TD mimics him. "Good morning, Siri."

"Morning. Did y'all have a successful trip?"

Charlie replies then winks at TD. "Yes, we did. Did you miss us?"

I roll my eyes at them.

TD chimes in. "Of course she did. Right?"

"Umm hmm." I lie.

Charlie, who thinks he is a serious playboy, is in his 30's but tells everyone he is 25. Tall, dark and handsome, I'm sure, have always been used to describe him. He is physically fit and a stud by most standards. I catch him staring at me from his office a lot. I've seen his type in Vegas. *He would be a regular in the VIP lounge.* He grew up here, graduated college, moved back home, was hired by Mr. Connors, and has worked here since.

Then there is TD, short for Thomas David, but he tells everyone, it's short for Touch Down. TD, who has a serious case of hero worship on Charlie, is barely 21. Short, pale and cute, I'm sure, have always been used to describe him. He has shoulder length, white blonde hair, deep blue eyes, salon tanned skin and slightly crooked, but very white teeth. He is a transplanted, metro man that blow dries his hair with a big brush to give it a little extra body and manicures his nails. He left college early, then couldn't find a job. His mother called in a favor from Mr. Connors and he was hired. As soon as I met him I knew he was another spoiled, rich kid and a Mama's boy. I've seen his type in Vegas too. I don't care for them very much, but their money is as green as everyone else's and they usually tip extravagantly because it isn't their own hard, earned money. TD is no exception. He drives a fire red Porsche. *Nuff said.*

The phone rings. "Run along, you two. Someone around here has to work." I tell them as I shoo them away. Turning my back on them, I answer it as they each go into their offices.

It's Charlie's young wife, Mandy. "Siri, hey, this is Mandy." She whispers. "Don't tell Charlie I called. I want to surprise him. Is he in yet?"

"Yes ma'am. That's right."

She giggles. "Good. I went shopping and have a new outfit to show him."

"He'll like that."

She giggles again. Mandy is barely 20. "Is TD in too?"

"Yes ma'am. That's right."

"Good. My outfit will make his eyes pop out of his head." She giggles so hard she can barely breathe.

It makes me chuckle despite my professional attitude. "He would enjoy that very much. Will you be stopping by later on to demonstrate your products?"

"Oh, you are good, Siri. Yes, I'm on my way now. Charlie was gone 5 days! I need a good fucking."

"Yes ma'am. Please don't describe it to me. Save your sales pitch for him."

She giggles again. "I like you, Siri."

"Likewise, ma'am. See you soon." I hang up the phone and doodle a pretend note. *I could really make this budding threesome awesome. TD wants Mandy, Mandy wants TD, and Charlie wants to watch. I might just write Mandy the note when I leave.*

I think back to TD's first day. Mandy surprised Charlie with an afternoon fuck. She popped in, did Charlie, then popped out. TD came out of his office in time to see her climb into her baby blue Mazda

Miata, pick her recently acquired, enormous tits up and position them so she could steer and drive away.

"DAMN!" He said as he stared out the window. Charlie came out of his office, strolled to the water cooler, poured himself a cup, sipped it slowly, then turned to look at TD. The two men exchanged a long, meaningful look. TD started to grin and Charlie grinned too. They both returned to their offices without saying a word.

I watch for Mandy's Miata to pull in the lot, but she never shows. *Something unexpected must have happened. I hope she is alright.*

The phone rings breaking my thoughts. "Connors Chemical Corporation. This is Siri. How may I direct your call?"

"Siri, this is Mandy. My mom stopped by. I won't be able to come in this morning after all." She sounds like she has been crying.

"I'm sorry to hear that. Is there anything I can do?"

"No. I just wanted you to know. Thanks."

Hanging the phone up, I stare at it concerned. She is always so happy and bubbly. To think she has been crying breaks my heart. I immediately think of Lei. She came from an abusive family, but she made a better life for herself and she enjoys that life to the fullest. Mandy is a lot like Lei. Charlie snatches open his office door and as he hurries out. "I won't be back today. Something unexpected has come up."

Good. Go to your wife. She needs you. "Ok."

I skip lunch like I do most days the men are in the office. Too much 'harmless' flirting goes on here and I do my best to ignore it all. TD comes out of his office several times in the afternoon to chat me up, but I manage to look too busy and not available. At the end of the day, I walk back to Mr. Connors office, knock. When no one answers, I leave my payroll evaluation papers and timecard in his inbox, outside his door, along with a Thank You letter for allowing me the opportunity to be a part of his company. *Tomorrow is my last day. Yay!*

At 3:45, I straighten my desk, then daydream out the window of Moore, waiting for 4 o'clock sharp. *The plan tonight to see him is simple. I will listen at my door for him to leave and I will go down to my car with him. I hope he made it home ... safe. ... alone.* I check the time again, impatient for the day to be over.

Suddenly, TD comes out of his office in a full blown panic. He is truly upset. I jump and put my hand to my heart. "TD, you scared me! What's wrong? Is it Mandy?"

He doesn't hear me. He rants as he paces back and forth. "God dammit! Rachael. You Bitch! You can't cancel now! There isn't enough time to find someone else! God dammit!" He puts his fingers in his mouth and chews his manicured finger nails, then starts pacing again. "I finally get an invitation to the cocktail party tomorrow night and you dump me the day before? Fuckin' cunt, some friend you are! That's just like you, leaving me high and dry!" He runs his fingers through his hair. "What am I going to do?" I listen as he blows off steam talking about how he needs this invitation to be included in their circle of friends. The local big money boys. Then he turns on his heel, walks over to my desk, puts both hands on it, and leans toward me. "What are you doing tomorrow night, Siri? Would you consider going with me?"

"No." I answer automatically. He throws his hands up, spins around and starts pacing again. He turns to me and begs. "PLEASE! I'm desperate here! I have to have a date. I can't go alone and I don't know anyone else in this fucking hell hole! Please!" He gets down on his knees, crawling to me. "Pretty please! With sugar on top and all that shit girls want to hear." When he reaches me, he tries to take my hand.

I pull it away and wave him off, laughing at him. "Get up! Someone will see you and get the wrong idea."

His eyes light up. "If you don't say you'll go, I'm going to run to the back offices and tell everyone we fucked up here on your desk."

"Ha! I don't give a shit what any of them think of me." He looks like he is going to cry. His bottom lip starts to tremble as he looks away completely dejected.

My gut screams "NO" when I make my decision, but I hate to see a grown man cry. I hate to see anyone cry. "I will go as your colleague."

"Oh, thank you, thank you, thank you!" He rushes towards me.

"Whoa, whoa, whoa. Stop right there." I throw my hands up to block him.

He stops his advance, but reaches for my hand, trying to kiss it. I wave him away. "Don't kiss up, TD! It's not manly."

He turns around, puts his hands under his hair, fluffs it, then runs his fingers through it to settle down the fly aways and regain his composure.

"But… and this is a BIG but! Are you listening?"

He looks at me. "Yes. I'm listening. But?"

"BUT this is NOT a date. I'm only a stand in for the girl who cancelled. I am not a friend. I am a colleague, doing another colleague a favor. That's all! This is NOT a date. AND…."

"NOT a date. No problem. Got it! And?"

"I have one rule."

"Ok. I can handle a rule. What is it?"

"Rule #1: No touching!"

He laughs. "Really? NO touching? I thought you were going to say I can't drink and drive."

"No touching! None, nix, nada, null, zero on the touching."

"Deal." He sticks his hand out for me to shake.

I raise my eyebrows. "Really? Did you think I would fall for that? No touching means NO touching."

He smiles down at me with a crooked smile that looks like Charlie's playboy smile. "But my name is TD. That stands for Touch Down, Baby. Women can't resist my charms. I always score!"

I smile sweetly up at him with complete confidence. "Your name is Thomas David. And I'll be your first rejection. Don't be a shit!"

He puts his hands up covering his chest and backs away playing the charming misunderstood douche. "No foul!"

"Don't underestimate me, TD. No touching means no touching and I will enforce it."

He laughs. "Yeah right!" He spins away on his heel, taking off to his desk. I leave it at that because it's 4 o'clock and I'm out of here.

When I pull into the parking lot, the Raptor is there. As I park in my spot alongside it, Moore comes out of the building. My heart flips and instantly a smile is on my face. *I won't ever get tired of seeing his handsome self!* Then, it dawns on me. *He's leaving earlier today! I almost missed him!* I sit in my car watching him walk to me, waiting to greet him at his truck. As soon as he sees me, he smiles and heads straight to my door. He opens it for me, offering his hand to help me out. I take it and enjoy the tingle as I swing my legs like a lady, knowing I could easily give him a glimpse of my diva-ness, but not wanting to give him too much too early, and knowing if his thunder showed, I would give it up right here. I give him my most beautiful smile. "Hi."

"Hi. Did you have a nice day at the office?" He pulls me to my feet.

"It was ok. Tomorrow's my last day. I've had enough of the boring life."

He frowns and slightly squeezes my hand. "Are you leaving?"

"No, just the job. I'm going to hang around here a little while longer."

He smiles. "Glad to hear that. I thought for a minute you were going to say you were leaving for Vegas next week." He is still holding my hand and my skin is tingling so bad it tickles.

"That was the original plan but I changed my mind recently. I have some unfinished business to attend to. Some rain-checks to cash in."

His thumb strokes my fingers as his smile turns into a grin. He pulls me to him and closes my door. We stand there looking into each other's eyes and the electricity starts to build. My eyes drop to his lips. *I want to kiss him so bad!* The grin falls off his face and I look up to see his hungry expression. Then he looks past me to my car and steps around me. My hand falls out of his grasp. The tingling stops instantly. The thought of reaching for his hand crosses my mind but he walks up to my car and puts his hand on her. "This really is quite an extraordinary car."

I walk to stand next to him. "Yes, it is. Thanks." I run my fingers over my Ford Shelby GT500 lovingly, stroking her. "Most people don't realize that I drive an extraordinary car. They only see the Mustang body style."

"I'm not like most people." He smiles completely confident. His gaze leaves the car and looks me in the eye. "This baby has a lot of muscle under the hood. Can a petite, sweet, young, Wild Thang handle it?"

I like you, Moore. You are a lot of fun! Laughing, I take a side step and bump him. "I may be petite, and yes, I'm both sweet and young, but I assure you, I can handle the muscle under the hood." I drop my eyes to his crotch as I put my hands under my hair and pull it up. "Fast and furious, letting it scream." I release my hair, letting it fall, then swing it to the side and look at him. "Or nice and slow, making it moan, but either way, it will be a wild ride." I wink at him.

His eyes darken and the hungry expression is back. He opens his mouth to say something, but his iPhone plays "Same Love" by Macklemore. I raise my eyebrows, completely surprised by that. My expression makes him laugh and the sexual tension is gone. "My sister." He explains as he answers it. *Obviously a lesbian.* "What Baby Sister? Yes! I'm still coming." He rolls his eyes at me and laughs. "I'll be there in a little while. Chill out! I ran into a friend. I love you too." He hangs up. *This man is awesome! Not only is he unashamed to proclaim she is gay, but he easily says I love you to his 'Baby Sister!'* My heart feels a tug. "I have to go." He smiles and reaches for my hand.

I give it to him and the spark is back. "So I heard." He closes the distance between us and his expression is the sincere one. I look at him from under my eyelashes. *I really want a kiss!* Then my stomach growls really loud! Mortified, I close my eyes.

He laughs. "Sounds like you need to go eat."

"Yeah. I'm hungry."

"How about another raincheck?"

"Sure. For what?"

"A ride in your car. My choice of fast and furious or nice and slow." He squeezes my hand and leans toward me. I turn my face up for his kiss, but his sister calls back and "Same Love" blasts us, breaking the spell. We laugh looking into each other's face. He takes a step back, drops his head, and shakes it. "I can't catch a break." He hits ignore on his phone.

I squeeze his hand and step forward quickly to him. "I would love another raincheck. Your choice. Fast and furious or nice and slow." He smiles one of his sexy as hell smiles making me tingle. *Kiss me... right now!* But his phone goes off again. "I can't catch a break either." We both laugh, then I spin him around and push him towards his truck. "Go. It must be really important."

"My calendar is clear on Sunday. If not before …" Once in the truck, he puts the window down.

"Def on Sunday then."

"See ya Wright." He answers his phone, puts it in reverse and backs out.

I wave. "Ciao!" Then I turn and walk to our building. *I like you, Moore.*

Once in my apartment, I strip, put on a lace only robe, fix myself a salad and go out on to the balcony to eat it. *I'm starving.* I munch on my lettuce thinking about Moore. I start to laugh. *I don't even know his first name! Ok. That's priority #1. I don't want to call him Moore anymore. Besides, I can't find him on Facebook without it. How else am I going to stalk him and find out more intimate details about his life? I have to learn more about Moore.* I take a bite and chew. *See if he's on Tinder or OKCupid.com, or even Match.com!*

I finish my salad, take the bowl to the sink, and wash it. *What am I going to call him? The only thing that fits is Golden God. Nothing else really suits him. I'll call him that for now.*

Back out on the balcony, I download the apps, enter a quick description of myself, hit search, and … *nope, no Golden God Moore.* He isn't on any of them. *It was a long shot.* I give it up and decide to go in to work on the dance moves for "Happy," but I leave the doors open so I can listen for his Raptor to come back. I get my MacBook Pro, set it up on the chair in my converted living room and get to work. The video has so many components, it will be extremely complex, plus it will be a big theatrical challenge, but I think I can pull it off.

"Notes: Find a hat identical to Pharrell's." *It's perfect to stuff my hair in.* "Make sure Bart also gets up with Steve Carell, Kelly Osbourne, Jimmy Fallon and any other celebrity in the video for guest appearances. Work out some bait and switch moves to incorporate going in and out of Pharrell's character to the dancers that would be believable. Call a magician in to help with that." *The hardest portion will be doing the dude that kicks his legs doing a head stand then pushes up to one hand. If I can nail it, that guy's move alone should bring the house down. Especially when they discover I was performing the whole fucking thing. This video performance should sky rocket my show back to the top.* "Discuss bringing in the choreographer to help." *They don't get enough recognition.* "DO MORE HAND STAND PUSH-UPS!"

By the time I hear the Raptor pull into the parking lot, I have memorized the first portion of the video and I am doing the third set of hand stand push-ups on the wall. My arms feel like noodles, but I'm feeling stoked! I walk out onto the balcony to watch him park. He looks up to me immediately and waves as he walks in front of the headlights. I wave back. Once he is in the building, I shut my balcony doors, turn my computer off and go to bed. I fall back on it exhausted. *Tomorrow is my last day at work and then the cocktail party. After that, I will pursue the Golden God down the hall.* I fall asleep easily and dream of a golden statue that comes alive and carries me up to Mount Olympus, but not the one in the clouds. The one in Vegas.

CHAPTER FIVE

Thank God It's Friday is the first thought I have when I wake up, stretch my arms over my head and take three deep breaths. *I slept like a baby.* I go through my daily routine of stretches, but I skip the hand stand and push-ups. *I did enough of those last night.*

When I arrive at work, TD is there waiting on me. He opens the front door. "I have to go to the other office today. There's an issue I have to deal with. Let me have your digits. I'll pick you up at 7. The cocktails are at 8."

"No. I'm not giving you my personal number. You can use Facebook if you need to contact me."

"Fine. The attire is semiformal. Wear something more revealing." He looks at my breasts. "You do have something sexier than the business suits you always hide in, don't you?" He looks at my face and finds a severe smirk on it. "Wear something sexier." He opens the door, takes a step out, then backtracks. "Pretty please with sugar on top." His charm turned on high. "And thanks colleague."

"Sure. You're welcome."

My last day is uneventful. At 4 o'clock, I hug the few people who bothered to come by to wish me well. I'm glad the day is finally over. As I pull out of the parking lot for the last time, I thank my lucky stars that I went to Vegas and became a dancer instead of an Accountant.

Sitting at a red light, my phone vibrates. *That has to be TD.* *The cocktail party has been pushed to 10. Something about a flight being delayed. I'll pick you up at 9:15. If that's ok? Please let it be ok, with some sprinkles on top.*

I smirk at my phone. *He is pouring it on thick!* *It's ok. 9:15 then. The gate will be closed. I'll let the guard know to let you in. Make sure you have your driver's license. They will check your id after 9.*

When I pull into the parking lot, I see that Moore is gone. *Fuck! I need my Golden God fix for the day. And I need to find out his first name!*

Half way to the elevator, I remember TD and the gate. *I'll ask Mrs. Smith to let Tony know when he comes in.* At the office door, I see Lucy sitting at the desk. She is a small Asian woman about the same age as Mrs. Smith who handles the collections and evictions while Mrs. Smith is the people person. She is looking over some papers. *I hope the woman who was crying isn't getting evicted. I need to remember to chat Mrs. Smith up about her. If she needs help with her rent, I could slip a money order under the door and get her out of a pinch.* When I knock, Lucy looks up and smiles at me. "Hello Lucy. It's good to see you." She nods, but doesn't say anything. "Is Mrs. Smith around?"

"No." She goes back to studying the papers she has in her hand.

"Will she be back today?"

"No." Lucy speaks broken English with a heavy accent, but she understands it perfectly.

"Did her daughter have the baby?"

"Yes." Lucy smiles at me. "A gurl."

"Oh, that's wonderful! I know she is thrilled!"

"Yes. You need hep?"

"Yes. I have a visitor coming around 9:15. I wanted to let Tony know. I don't want to give this guy the gate code."

"OK. I tell Tony. Car?"

"He will be in a red Porsche."

"Ah, fancy. Good! You need life."

I laugh.

"You go out? Dat good. I tell Tony."

"Thanks."

In my apartment, I strip, throw on a tank top and yoga shorts. *I have four hours to kill. I'll call Cat later. Maybe she can talk.*

I grab my iPhone, a beer from the fridge, and go out on to the balcony. I plop down in my lounge chair to relax, run the beer across my forehead. I take a long drag on the bottle. *Ah! There is nothing like the first taste of an ice cold beer on a hot humid day.* I sing Halo softly to myself as I text Cat. *call me when you can talk a little while*

Laying my head back to enjoy the sun, and slowly sipping my brew, my thoughts return to Moore. *Yay! It's the weekend of Moore and me.* I grin wickedly at the sky. *I can't wait to explore him. Yum, I can't wait to run my hands over that fine fucking muscle.* My palms itch thinking of his hot golden skin with the soft golden hair and how it will tickle as I slide them over it. I suck hard on the bottle. *I wonder how big his penis is. I hope it isn't extra large. I've seen small pythons before. Lei says they are a bit much even for her. My guess is 6 to 8 inches. And I'm sure he knows how to wield it!* My hand slides down between my legs and rubs my pussy. *I can't wait to feel him in me! I'm horny as hell for him! Stop!* I stand up before I start masturbating. *I want the fucking fireworks finale!*

Leaning against the rail looking out over the parking lot, I finish my beer. "Brick House" starts to play. *Cat!* I pounce on my phone. "Hey girlie!"

"Hey baby girl!" The sound of her voice washes over me and makes me homesick for her. "Are you calling with details on the Flyboy?"

"Yeppers."

"I can't wait to hear. But first, how's your mother?"

"She's good as new. As soon as the doctors released her, she and Daddy left for a sailing trip around the Virgin Islands."

"That's great news. Does that mean you are coming back?"

"Yes, but not right away. I want to check out Moore."

"I understand. The heart wants what the heart wants. I have about 15 minutes to spare. Tell me all about this Flyboy named Moore."

"Well, first off, he isn't a Flyboy any more. I found out he has resigned."

"Whew! That's good. One less thing for the heart to deal with."

"Yep."

"So…. Come on, don't make me ask 20 questions. Spill it!"

I giggle. "Man, Oh, Man, Cat! He is absolutely gorgeous! He is the most beautiful man I have ever laid eyes on."

"Wow! That's really saying something. Better than the boys from Chippendales and the Thunder from Down Under?"

"Well, he stacks up. He literally makes my mouth water looking at him."

She laughs at that. "Give me a reference? Someone I can visualize! Tom Cruise in his flight suit in Top Gun has been floating around in my mind ever since I heard he was a pilot."

"Oh, no, he's better than Cruise. Think Thor, Chris Hemsworth."

"Who?" Cat pauses for emphasis then laughs. "No, I'm only kidding. *Damn!*"

"I know, right?"

"He has blonde hair then?"

"No. Yes. It's dark blonde with a few golden sun streaks that glisten."

"Well, that totally rules out Tom Cruise."

I laugh. "Well he has the great ass."

"We do love a great ass. How are his eyes and his smile?"

"Perfect!"

"No, what color are his eyes?"

"Emerald Green! When the light shines on them, they are bright emerald green."

"Damn! That's as rare as your light crystal green ones."

"He takes my breath away."

"No doubt. Do I even need to ask about his smile now?"

"It's prefect too! It lights up his face. You can think Tom Cruise there. And his eyebrows are dark, almost black too. They match the darker hair underneath."

"Ok, I'm thinking Brad Pitt now?"

"Who?" I tease her, pausing then laughing. "Just kidding! No, he's not like Pitt. I'll snap a pic as soon as I can and send it to you."

"So, let me get this right, you have found a man with emerald green eyes framed by dark brows, capped with a head of dark, yet golden, sun streaked hair on a body like Thor's?"

"YES! He is a fucking fine feast!"

"Wow! You better hook up with this guy. I can't wait to meet him now! Send me a pic ASAP." She speaks to someone on her end. "Hang on, Babe, I'll be there in 10 minutes." Then returns to me. "Sorry about that. We have a new girl coming in to train, and I need to watch her skills. You know the drill. How much is she going to need before we can put her on the floor?"

"Yeah, I remember my two weeks of intense torture at your hands." I laugh.

"You were the easiest one I ever taught, sweetie. Not everyone has your natural ear for music and your raw dance talent."

"I thought Laura was doing your training?"

"She's pregnant! I didn't text you?"

"No! Oh my gosh! How did that happen?"

"Unprotected fucking. It only takes one time. Don't you get caught! Too many people depend on your dancing for their living."

"Don't worry, Cat, I've taken precautions. I'm not about to fuck up this dream I call my life. It's too sweet. So, has she left and gone back home?"

"No, she is still working for me. I'm training her as a manager now. We have basically traded jobs. You hate to lose good girls, you know? And she's more like family."

"Yeah, I know." I feel a twang of guilt at not returning immediately, but I know I can't until Moore is either more, or no more. "I'm sorry! I didn't ask how the club is doing. How's it going? How are the girls, and Bart?" I roll my eyes at myself. "I'm so caught up in this guy, I can't think straight."

Cat laughs at me. "You're in love, girl! And you don't even know his name! But we're ok. We're still rolling in the dough, living the dream, but we miss you. Customers are starting to rotate back in too and they are asking when Surreal will perform again."

"I know. Give me a couple more weeks, and I promise to return to Vegas. I'll know by then one way or the other on Moore."

"I'm going to hold you to that. As a matter of fact, I'll have Bart schedule his jet to pick you up. Let's say on May 1st. May day!"

"Ok, I promise to be on it when it returns. Come hell or high water." I hear her cracking up at my southern lingo. "Give Bart a squeeze for me. Tell him, my green eyes are goo-goo over this guy."

"I know exactly what he will say. 'Tell her to get her glowing green eyes back here or he'll be goo-goo! And if that man breaks her heart, I'll personally come down there and make his eyes goo-goo!'"

We both crack up at the thought of Bart even using the term goo-goo. He is much too sophisticated for lingo like that. "Hey, before you go, I wanted to tell you I'm going out tonight. To a cocktail party. A colleague from work was supposed to go with someone else, but she canceled on him at the last minute. He begged me to take her place. He was so desperate, I agreed."

"That's fantastic! What are you wearing? Did you buy a new dress?"

"No, I didn't have time. He asked me yesterday afternoon."

"Good! You are going to wear your Black & Blue Baby! It will remind you of who you are! You are not a hick from the sticks. You are our gold mine. Our million dollar, Baby Girl. Surreal! Star! The toast of Vegas! I know what you are thinking. It's possible someone has seen your show and might put two and two together, but as your manager, that's a chance I want you to take. Please, please, tell me you will wear it!"

"I'm so glad you approve. It's too Diva for around here, but it's all I have."

"The wives will be shocked, but the men will love it. They always have. Are you still working on your pole routines?"

"All the time. It's all I do in my infinite amount of spare time. I've become addicted to exercise!"

"Don't get too lean and toned now. Keep your curves!"

"I'm not. Don't worry. I've been developing some new routines for Seary and I'm working on a killer return performance for Surreal to 'Happy.'"

"Pharrell's 'Happy?'"

"Yes! I have an idea that will send my return to the top of the strip."

"I can't wait to see it! Have you seen Beyoncé's 'Partition' video?"

"Yes, I've been doing it too. It's ready to go." I walk to the stripper pole. I remember Mrs. Smith's raised eyebrows when I asked about having it installed, but Bart is right, 'Money talks and shit walks.'

"That's fantastic. I'll tell Bart to clear it with Beyoncé's people."

"If I can't get the kinks worked out on 'Happy,' I can do 'Partition' and save 'Happy' for the 4th of July. It will be the biggest production yet. I've got some really cool ideas. I'll email James my production thoughts so he can start working on it. But let's not blab about that. How's the girls? I miss them."

"They miss you too. Lola and Red, both asked when you were coming back this morning. Everyone misses your giggles including me. The dressing room and practice sessions haven't been the same without your silliness."

"What? No one else cuts up or just busts loose?"

"No! It's gotten more and more serious without you. Hurry home! That's an order! I need laughter!"

"How's Lei doing?"

"She's been doing great. I think you've officially saved another one. She's taken over your role as mood monitor and she'll sing 'Beautiful' or 'Invisible' to anyone who even remotely looks sad, much less depressed. She doesn't have the voice you do, but her heart is in the right place. It's really very touching, Siri. You would be proud."

"I can't tell you what that means to me." I tear up. "Give her a squeeze from me."

"I will. Listen, you know I have to run. It was so good to hear your voice. Take care of yourself. I'll let everyone know we are having a party when you get back."

"I will. I can't either! I need some hugs! I'm home sick for y'all."

"Love you, Baby Girl."

"Love you too! Bye Cat!"

I hang up. *Gosh, it was so good to talk to Cat. I miss her and my life. I'm ready to go home! I am ready to be back in the spotlight. I miss dancing and performing! I miss Vegas!*

My iPhone dings and the invitation from Cat for May 1, 2014 is there. "The jet will arrive at 3 o'clock your time. Have your bags packed! You're coming home!" I smile at my phone. *She is so organized!*

My stomach growls. *Time to eat.* I grab a chicken salad and a water then go back out on the balcony to eat. I pig out as I listen to all the parking lot traffic. When I'm done, I drink my water as I try to guess Moore's first name. *Nothing fits him. He doesn't look like a Michael, or a Richard, or even a*

Lee. I shake my head. *Nothing fits him.* Back in the kitchen, I throw my meal away, grab another water then return to the balcony. *I have to find out what his damn name is!* When I step out, I hear his truck. It has a distinct sound, like purring. I walk to the edge of the railing to watch him. *How do you properly dream about someone without calling them by their first name? Easy. You call him a Golden God.* I smirk. *If the shoe fits.*

I watch the Golden God park his truck. The spot next to my car is taken. He has to find another, but he finds one closer. When he gets out, he leans over the side of the truck bed. He is wearing a big armed, black tank top over a pair of plaid shorts and flip flops. The view even from this distance of his golden hair, broad shoulders, perfect skin and perfect ass causes that sweet lurching feeling as my pussy tightens involuntarily. He stands up with two bags of groceries and a case of beer. *He's been to the grocery store.* I can see more grocery bags in the bed. *He cooks too? This guy just keeps getting better and better.*

As he walks toward our building, he looks up to my balcony smiling. *You know I watch for you.* I wave then twirl around humming "Halo" again ready to find out what his name is. Going to my closet for my shoes, I slip into a pair of wedge sandals and pause looking at my reflection. My nipples are standing out happy at the thought of seeing him. *Shit! I don't have a bra on!* For the sake of time, I throw a t-shirt over the tank and head out the door. My plan is simple. *Get his name! I will be standing at the elevator door when it opens. I will say ... something! He will say something. I will tell him my name, and he will tell me his. There you go, perfect!*

When I step out into the hall, I see Lucy walking toward me. "Shit! Not now!"

She throws her hand up in a wave to me. "Miss Wright, I toll Tony, ok?"

"Ok, that's great. Thanks so much."

"I speak with you."

"Yes, of course. I was heading down to my car. Can we discuss it on the way down?"

"No."

The elevator dings and I hear the doors slide open. *Shit!* Moore exits looking so fucking fine in that tank top. He completely fills out the large arm holes with his immense chest and bulging back. He pauses to look down the hall to my apartment, but when he sees me standing outside with Lucy, he turns away heading to his place with his groceries. I watch his retreating figure over the top of Lucy's head.

She turns to see who I am gawking at then turns back frowning. "No. We talk here. Now."

"Now? Lucy, it's Friday afternoon. Can't we do it another day, another time?"

"No. Now."

I open my door and invite her in. *There were at least 2 more bags. He has to make another trip. All is not lost. Don't panic. But hurry!*

"When you go, we fix dis." She walks into the living room and stands by the stripper pole.

"Yes, I already paid to have the apartment returned to the original state." I head back to my door and wait for her. "We're good, aren't we?" I open the door for her.

"No. Not good. You pay rent too.

"Rent?" I hear the elevator ding. I stick my head out the door in time to see Moore walk in. *I've only got a couple of minutes to ditch Lucy.* I look back to see that she has crossed the apartment and is standing next to me at the door.

"Rent at repair."

"Oh! I understand. I have to pay rent the month they are fixing it back."

"Yes." She nods and looks stern at me.

"Ok, I will pay it too."

"Ok den." She smiles and follows me into the hallway.

As I start to walk down to the elevator I see that she is still standing at my door. "Is there something else?"

"When you pay?"

"I'll pay it with this month's rent, if that's good." I am walking backwards towards the elevator.

She nods. "Yes. Good." She points to my door knob. "We change dis too. No keys."

"Ok. Great."

"You in big hurry?"

"Yes, actually I am."

"Ok din." She walks away from my apartment. "We like parking idea too."

"Good." I slow down and wait for her to catch up.

"You get two free." She smiles at me.

"That's fantastic. Thanks."

"Umm hmm."

When we get to the elevator, I ask. "Are you going down or up?"

"Down too."

I push the down button. *Shit! She's going to be standing here when he gets off.* We stand there in silence waiting for the elevator to arrive. When it dings and the door opens, Moore steps out holding four bags of groceries.

His face lights up when he sees me. "Miss Wright." He speaks to Lucy too. "Good afternoon, Lucy. How are you today?"

"Fine, Fly Boy." There is clear animosity in her tone. She brushes him aside, knocking his bags out of the way and gets in the elevator.

He starts to say something else, but closes his mouth, stunned. *The look on his face is priceless.* I can't help but giggle. He winks at me and I stare after him, watching as he walks to his apartment.

Lucy holds the doors open for me. "You come." She commands me.

But what I hear is, 'you cum.' I whisper to myself. "I intend to." I rub my twitching palms down the fronts of my thighs, bending over slightly. Pushing my tits together, I smile at the motion of his perfect physique moving with perfect posture. His teres major and deltoid muscles are shown off by his tank top, but it's his ass that holds my eye. *His gluteus is maximus!* The whole package walking away makes me whisper. "The man truly walks like a fucking God!"

Lucy asks, "What you say?"

When he reaches his door, he shifts the bags to one hand, pulls out his key and looks back at me as he unlocks it. *Shit! Busted.* He grins and waits.

I grin and turn to Lucy. "Oh, I said, 'I've left my car keys, Oh my God.' You go on down without me."

"Umm hmm." She shakes her head as the elevator doors close. "Fly Boys, day no good."

When I turn back to Moore, he has gone inside. I sigh as I start walking backward to my apartment. *What if I walked down there, knocked and said, 'How about that bottle of wine now?' If I did that, I wouldn't be going to the cocktail party. Poor TD would cry for sure! Be patient. You didn't get Moore's first name, but you got a killer wink. One last obligation, then you can devote yourself totally to him. Finding out his name will pale in comparison to finding out what delights we will explore until May 1.*

CHAPTER SIX

Back in my bedroom, I hang my Black & Blue Baby on the closet door. "Girlie, we're going to go to a cocktail party tonight where you will make the men drool and the women secretly cream themselves. Then later, they will fuck until the sun rises and fall into a deep satisfied coma." Flopping backward on the bed, I bounce. "And on May 1st, we are flying home with or without Moore but I sure hope it is with Moore."

Home. Vegas. I stare at my dress in silence. *For three years I have called Vegas home. There are so many great memories tied up in this dress. I've entertained so many people! You know what I should do while I'm waiting? I should update my Facebook fan pages. I've been neglecting them.* I get my Mac Book Pro, and sitting with my legs in a yoga stretch on the bed, I open it to Facebook. I'm impressed every time I check my pages. The number of fans I have for Surreal is in the 100k's, but Seary has a very respectable 20,000. To think that a small town girl from the Deep South has made it so big in a place like Vegas is really overwhelming. I'm still the same little girl, but I'm so much more now. *I really have*

*an awesome support team surrounding me that
makes everything run smooth. I need to do something
special for them when I return to let them know how
much I truly appreciate all they do. Maybe I'll fly
everyone to Colorado for a few days.*

When I finish, I check the time. It's 8 o'clock.
Time to get ready.

After my shower, I apply a light brush of silver
with a tad of smoky navy at the corners of my eyes.
That will be enough to make my green eyes pop.
Walking back to my closet to get dressed, I strut
knowing I will turn heads, harden cocks, and wet
pussies.

*It will feel good to be a Diva again. Cat was
right.* I lovingly step into my Black & Blue Baby,
then lean over so my boobs fall forward, pull the
specially designed bodice in place and close the
miniature quick snap on the collar. When I straighten
up everything settles into place perfectly.

The diamond shaped bodice has a tight choker
style collar of super soft black leather. There are no
sleeves and no back. It is made of a special blend of
spandex and micro fiber in indigo blue and contains a
large heart shaped hole cut in the bosom. The top
point of the heart lays at the top of my cleavage, flat
against my breast bone. It then goes up and out,
rounds inward, barely missing my nipples and ending

in a point at the bottom of my cleavage. Hidden in the lining are push-up pads which keep my breasts plump in the heart hole and on full display. A heavy black braid forms a bigger heart around the rest of the bodice. It starts at the top of the open heart, but the sides of this heart go down the outside of my tits, hugging them and also serving to keep everything in place while I maneuver on the pole. The sides move inward above my waist, traveling down below my navel, and finishing in a point at my hidden Lovers Heart.

I hear Cat's training voice. *No one is immune to the sexual arousal tits stir within. No one!* The dress was designed so that when I strut, my DD's jiggle with a grace all their own. *Like an ocean wave, the eyes are spell bound. They can't look away.*

The super short, super soft, black leather skirt also forms the shape of a heart both in the front and in the back. The heart point in the front starts where the black heavy braid ends. It arches up over my hips, then around to the back, where it hugs my full, firm ass like a glove. Laying on the tops of my butt cheeks, the top point of the heart in the rear sits at the crack of my ass. The hem line, in the front and back, is cut at an angle so that only half of a bottom point is made, but the impression is of another heart shape. From the back, the only fabric you see is what is covering my ass. The cut, the lay, and the design makes the fabric move when I strut in my stiletto's with each cheek rolling, like a heart beating.

The whole dress is a fucking work of art! Instantly, I feel like the million dollar baby I am. The final touch is my black leather stilettos. Which I slip into, then roll up in a classic stripper move. *And I'm feeling good!*

As Surreal, I always wear my thick hair down with massive big curls, streaked with blue and black hair paint, and laced with gold. It's very dramatic, very fly! To conceal my face and protect my identity, I wear a belly dancer veil and full mardi gras mask. *But tonight, I'll wear my hair up, in a simple French twist.* I dig around the dresser for my invisible clip. Starting at the nape of my neck, I form the simple knot then tuck the ends in and secure it. When I look in the mirror, it hangs softly. *Now, to pull out a few, small, long strands around the nape and ... wha la, an air of elegance while remaining cool and sexy.*

Now the only problem is a handbag. A heavy strap will interfere with my cleavage, but I'm not going off with TD without protection. I wonder if I brought my black leather Gucci. It has an extra-long, thin strap, I can lay along the heavy braid and keep my cleavage open or it can double as a clutch. I find it packed in one of the emergency suitcases. When I open it, I discover there is $1000 in a money clip from the last time I carried it. *Now for my info mini clutch,* which contains my driver's license and a couple of credit cards. I drop it in and check the time on my phone. It's 9:00. *Perfect timing.*

I sit on the bed and reach under my pillow. And *last but not least;* I pull out my Ruger LCR, check the bullets in the chamber, make sure it is secure and drop it in. *Brutus, you would be so proud of me for remembering.*

Walking into the kitchen, I lay the purse down on the counter. Taking my phone, I walk to the balcony to watch for TD. I quickly text Cat. *Tell Brutus I want him on that May 1st flight coming to pick me up. I miss the big ole boy.*

I quickly scan the parking lot. *Now to wait for TD, get some good karma for doing this, and move forward with my pursuit of happiness and the Golden God.* I feel the vibration of a text. *He's already on the flight manifest. :-)* I smile as I step to the railing and drink in the evening air. The Raptor hasn't moved. *I wonder if Moore is having friends over for dinner. He had enough food for several people. Maybe I'll pretend to be locked out tonight and knock on his door when I come back.*

At exactly 9:15, I see TD's car enter the lot. I close the French doors and lock up. "Show time!"

Grabbing my purse, I stuff my phone in it then lock the door behind me and drop in the key. Walking down the hallway to the elevator, I strut with all the sass I feel, all dressed up again. Boobs bouncing. Ass beating. I focus on 9G and try to will Moore to come out. *I want to see you! I want you to see me!*

At the elevator, I push the down button. It dings and the doors slide open almost immediately. Entering, I realize the gun is just a little too heavy to carry in my hand. *I don't want to drop it.* I pull the strap free and hang it over my head and shoulder as I move to the back corner. The weight of the gun makes it hang nice. I roll my shoulder around testing it. *That's good.*

As the doors start to slide closed on their own, my eyes focus on the shrinking gap and my mind flashes to the views of Moore I've had through them. Our special connection emphasized there. *I want to see him... now.* Right on cue, a golden hand slides in, stopping their progress.

Fuck yeah! My heart flip flops, skips a couple of beats, then races to my throat, choking off my air. The butterflies return, circling, making every part of me tingle. Instantly, I'm turned on.

His hand rests on the door as they stop and reverse their path. *Now that's a real man's hand.* His fingers are strong and nimble. His nails are clean and neatly cut.

As the doors open, I smile and silently mouth. "Sweet Zeus, Father of the Fucking Gods, Thank You." And when the gap is big enough for his frame to squeeze through, the most beautiful man I have ever laid eyes on slides in with his back to me, pulling his phone out of his front pants pocket and typing something with one hand, while holding a cooler, probably full of beer, in the other.

Tonight he is dressed in another J Crew shirt, short sleeves, loosely buttoned, with tight, white pants. The shirt is dark purple and his skin tone is warm against it. His hair reflects soft gold tints in the elevator light. Even the hair on his arms reflects gold highlights.

I smirk. *He doesn't see me! He is seriously preoccupied with his phone.* No one was in the hallway when he came out of his apartment and the elevator was standing open. *He thinks he is alone.* I grin as I watch him push the phone back in his pants pocket, then the L button on the elevator panel. As the doors close, I inhale deeply through my nose trying to be as quiet as a mouse. *Yum!* I close my eyes and they roll back into my head. *Old Spice cologne and his musk! He smells like heaven itself!*

The elevator starts its descent and he takes a step back as he sets the cooler down almost on my foot. I try to move it inconspicuously, but his eyes dart to the movement. When he sees my stilettos, his eyebrows raise and a slow, sexy smile spreads across his face.

I melt.

In slow motion, he turns, and his gaze crawls up my legs taking in every curve.

I tingle where they touch.

As he looks up my dancer legs, his expression changes from playful to hungry.

I am not breathing.

When he gets to the hem of my dress, he pauses as if he knows I'm naked under it.

I'm pinned to the wall.

His eyes linger at my pussy.

My clit throbs.

His gaze moves upward again. He enjoys my cleavage.

My heart pounds in my chest.

He examines my tits, taking in every detail.

I gulp a breath of air. My chest expands. The edges of my nipples flash him.

His thunder ripples across his face.

My chest heaves.

He watches it rise and fall.

I am quivering.

His eyes continue up my neck.

I am hot.

He studies my lips.

I lick them.

His emerald green, gorgeous eyes thunder into mine.

I am trembling inside.

He steps over the cooler and invades my space.

I am powerless to resist him.

His body heat floods the air.

I am on fire.

His breath caresses my face.

I nearly swoon.

He smells my hair. A low throat moan escapes him.

I tingle.

He looks back into my eyes. His thunder is there, raw, unguarded.

I turn my face away.

He puts his arms against the wall, encompassing me within his essence. "Hi."

I lick my lips again.

"Look at me."

I lift my face.

He smiles.

My eyes fall to his lips.

"Giorno e notte sogno solo di te."

I bite my lip hard.

The smile falls from his face. I sense his thunder lying just beneath the surface.

I feel ... wild!

The elevator slows, then dings and comes to a stop on the 5th floor. As the doors slide open, he moans.

"Oh...." We hear a surprised voice as someone enters the elevator.

Moore drops his arms, then turns to stand next to me, politely facing front. We both stare straight ahead. A middle aged man has entered but his wife has not. She takes one look at me gulping air, finally able to breathe, then looks at Moore. Her eyes fall to his groin and she reaches out for her husband's arm. "Go ahead. We will wait for the next one." The man grunts as she pulls him back out.

When the elevator starts down, I wait, wanting Moore to resume his seduction, but he doesn't. He stands firm beside me. "I guess you are going out tonight?"

"How could you tell?" My flirty tone is sweet and sassy.

He chuckles still staring forward. "With someone ... special?"

"No. Apparently, you're going out tonight with someone else."

He grins and turns to face me, resting his shoulder on the wall.

I grin and turn my face to him. "Are you going out with someone … special?"

He laughs. "No. I'm going alone to a Hail and Farewell on post. I don't know where the special someone in my life is going." He winks at me. "Where are you going?"

I laugh. "To a cocktail party with a colleague from my temp job. He had a last minute cancellation yesterday and I agreed to go with him so he wouldn't have to back out."

"So, a hot date?"

"No. *Not* a hot date!"

He closes the distance. His body heat hits me. "You sure look hot."

I look away as a flush falls over my skin. *You make me hot!*

He leans his head down and whispers in my ear. "You really look hot!" He runs his fingers down my arm. My skin feels scorched from his heat as goose bumps pop out. He smiles knowing his seduction is working.

The elevator dings and comes to a stop. As the doors slide open onto the lobby, he bows slightly and gestures. "After you, my lady."

I turn barely controlled wild eyes to him. "I *am* hot! Really hot." I wink at him as I exit. *Time to do a little seduction of my own.* Strutting my stuff across the lobby floor with the full swagger of a $1,000,000 Vegas star in her signature diva dress, I work it! *Try taking your eyes off this!* Half way across, he lets out a long, low whistle. I laugh softly at his reaction. *Moore, you are a rascal.*

I continue all the way to the exit doors before I glance back to see if he followed or not. He is still standing in the door of the elevator, blocking it, relaxed, watching me. *Fuck yeah, you look like a Golden God standing there so comfortable, enjoying the view, not the least bit intimated, in complete control of yourself and knowing you are capable of completely controlling me too. Damn straight. A real man!*

I stand expectantly at the door, waiting patiently, and give him a beautiful, sweet smile. He responds with his big beautiful smile, picks up his cooler and walks to me. I'm struck by how comfortable he is in his own skin. *He doesn't exude confidence exactly, it's really something more. More like competence.*

When he reaches me, he sticks out his hand. "It's time to formally introduce ourselves, Miss Wright." I slip mine into his. He allows my whole hand to slide into his deep grasp, engulfing it. He pulls me to him, making me take a step forward and invade his space. My passion flows with the touch of his skin and the closeness of his body, only the public lobby keeps it under control. He squeezes my hand, making me quiver. "Aurei Moore."

"Ari? Short for…?"

He smiles his sexy half smile. "Aurelius."

"Of course." I say as if it's quite common to meet a man named Aurelius in Alabama. *Aurelius. The last great Roman Emperor was Marcus Aurelius. My Latin is rusty, but Aureus is an adjective meaning "golden."* I smirk. *Yes, I knew you were Golden and a God of a man.* My eyes twinkle. *Aurelius fits you perfectly!*

"And your name, Miss Wright?"

"Siri."

"Siri?" He hums deep within his throat. "Interesting. Spelled?"

I cock my head narrowing my eyes questioning his response, but I answer. "S. I. R. I."

"Of course." He says using the same voice inflection as his eyes twinkle too, making me giggle instead of asking why he asked how I spell it. "Your name means beautiful woman who leads us to victory."

"Why … yes, it does." I grin surprised. "And Aurelius's Latin translation is Aureus meaning golden."

"Affirmative. That's Army talk for yep." He releases my hand and opens the door for me.

I giggle at his definition as I walk through the doorway.

He holds the door open for a couple of ladies going in. They tell him. "Thank you." And he answers. "Yes Ma'am."

Standing outside, I wait for him to join me. *Aurelius.* When he walks up, I smile at him. "Aurelius." I hum deep within my throat. "Interesting. Ari is spelled A.R.I. or A.U.R.E.I?"

He grins surprised. "A.U.R.E.I." Then he winks at me. "Good call, Siri." *That wink is killer!*

The night security lights are bright, illuminating the area as if it were a cloudy day. We stroll to the parking lot together, chatting. He walks close enough to me that his sleeve brushes my arm. I bump him, wanting to touch him any way I can. "So, you have resigned from the Army?"

"Yes, I gave them six good years, but I'm not a lifer."

"Do you think you will miss it?"

"No." He gives me a super sexy smile. "Not now. Now, La vita è bella." He translates immediately. "Life is beautiful. I'm feeling good, really good, about the decision to get out and hang around here now. I'm looking forward to a new life."

I smile back. "I know how you feel!" I look out in the parking lot, as I add casually bumping him again. "Life feels pretty fucking fantastic, right now."

He chuckles. "Yes, it does."

"Do you think you will miss flying?"

"No, I have my private pilot's license."

"Oh that's dope! Maybe you can take me for a flight sometime?"

At the curb, I step off, but he pauses. "I think that soaring with you is definitely going to happen." I squeeze my pussy and my jaw jets out as I suck my lips. *DEF! That is definitely going to happen.* Coming alongside me, his smirk turns into a blatant grin and mine matches it, as we let the innuendo tease the air.

When we step past the car parked in the first visitor spot, Aurei looks down the row and sees something that makes him stiffen, almost imperceptibly, but I notice it, so I lay my hand on his arm as I peek behind his back to see what it was that caused his reaction. It was TD. He is parked about 7 cars away, casually smoking a cigarette, sitting on the trunk of his Porsche. He is wearing really distressed jeans with a pale blue Christian D'or shirt and loafers. He has his long, white blonde hair French braided in a ponytail. He glances at us, thumps the cigarette into the parking lot and mouths "Sup" with a head nod, but he completely ignores us as he pulls another cigarette out of his pocket.

I roll my eyes. "Good Gawd! French braided hair? Really?"

Aurei chuckles. "You *do* have a hot date." He tells me as we walk to his Raptor.

"He thinks he's hot."

"That's not what I meant. There is no way that guy thinks *you two* are NOT on a hot date."

We arrive at the Raptor. "He would have asked any female, but he doesn't know anyone else."

Aurei raises his eyebrows and gives me a skeptical 'yeah right' look. "I believe *you,* but … mark my words, *he's* thinking *he* has a *hot* date with *you.*"

I laugh at his expression. "I'm a big girl. I can handle the likes of him. He knows it's only a favor."

"Are you *sure* he knows that?"

"I made it clear we are not on a date."

"Crystal?"

"Yes. Crystal clear. I only agreed because he was so pitiful and Karma has been very good to me. I need to pay her a small token of appreciation."

"You are such an interesting find, Wild Thang. A one of a kind."

I smirk at his nickname. "Yes. I won't deny I am unique."

He chuckles as he leans over the side of the truck with the cooler. "And so modest too."

"If it's true, you can say it, right?" My eyes fall to the view of his perfect fucking muscle displayed before me. *Um, um, um.* My hand tingles with an urge to caress it. *It is full, round, tight, powerful.* Thoughts of his fucking muscle in action stir my pent-up passion and in the privacy of the parking lot, it comes to the surface. My pussy lurches, my heart starts to pound, my breathing get shallow and I bite my lip as I run my palms over my hips to ease the sensation.

"That's affirmative." He looks over his shoulder at me.

I lift my eyes from his ass. My face has lost its playful flirting. *You are the man of my dreams, Aurelius Moore.*

He sets the cooler down in the truck bed, then moves to stand territorially between me and TD. He walks up until his shirt touches my breasts. His eyes crinkle.

I close my eyes as my tingling palms spread to tingling tits. I hear words whispered so softly that I'm not sure if it's him or my own thoughts. "It's true. Say it!" He is so close I can smell him without inhaling. *His scent is intoxicating.* My nipples tighten and elongate, trying to touch him. My insides are quivering.

"Look at me." His commanding tone makes me open my eyes and I find him smiling down at me. He whispers. "La donna dei miei sogni!" Being this close to his moving lips, my eyes can't resist them. *They are truly exquisite. Incredibly beautiful moving to form his whispers.* I catch glimpses of his tongue behind his teeth. *I like his lips. I would like his lips on my lips.*

The urge to push my hard nipples into his hard body or kiss his unsuspecting mouth, makes me lay my hand on his chest and push away gently to keep the little gap between us safe. He reaches up and clasps it. "No." He drags it down his torso and holds it by our sides. Shivers run through me, reconnected. "Don't push me away." His commanding tone and words surprise me. Not because they are commanding, but because I melt with them. *Those lips are made for kissing.* His tongue sneaks out and touches the corner of his mouth. It slides over his lips to the other side, wetting them. *He's thinking the same thing.*

"Siri." *My name sounds so sexy rolling off his tongue.*

He waits for me to find his eyes. "You are ...." He waits again until I focus on his words. "Simply...." He waits again until I'm listening to him. "Stunning." He puts his hand on my chin holding me captive, but there is no need. I am under his control. I squeeze his hand and bring my other one up to rest on his waist. *I'm not going anywhere.*

He gently tips my face backward as he steps up touching our bodies. My tits scream with delight and I arch my back pushing them into him. He forces my chin up until my neck straightens. He holds me steady as he repeats the words without hesitating, staring into my soul. "Siri, you are simply stunning." His deep voice drops on the word 'stunning' and I feel ... deep down inside where no one has ever been before ... I feel myself falling.

With each breath he takes, I feel his essence blow across my face. His eyes become my whole world. He vanishes the gap between our mouths. I can feel his breath caress my lips as I wait for his kiss.

He stops short ... not touching them ....

My heart stops beating, listening, waiting, wanting. My lips tingle.

He waits.

All of my senses are on high.

He blows his breath very softly between my parted lips. I feel it caress my tongue. *Fuck! I'm free falling!* I gasp his name. "Aurei." He moans from his throat and a wild urge surges through me. Pushing hard against his hold on my chin, I force my lips to his as his hand slides down my jaw, around my ear, cupping it, controlling me, allowing me to place my lips on his.

His kiss is gentle, soft, and firm, all at the same time. *He tastes as good as he smells.* I hold my lips there drinking in the moment and the sweet sensation. When I release his lips, I lay my head back into his strong hand as my body collapses on him. I stare into his eyes vulnerable and sincere. *I have been looking for you all my life. I had almost given up hope that I would ever find someone who could make me feel this way.*

As he reads my expression, he moves his hands. One slides his fingers between my fingers, cinching us tight. And the other, he slides from my ear into the strands of my hair, pulling. *You are a dangerous man, Aurelius Moore.* There is pain and pleasure. Tears well up in my eyes from both. His eyes focus on them and his expression turns fierce.

Looking into the depths of his eyes, I see uncertainty. I stroke his waist as I smile, confident and unintimidated. *I am not afraid of you. I can handle whatever thunder lies inside you.* I whisper. "Thanks ... for the compliment."

"Oh, Siri." He holds me tight with his hands, squeezing my fingers and my hair as he breathes on my face. He closes his eyes and we stand there, silent, quiet, still. I feel him relaxing, releasing his control. I move my free hand to his arm and he slides his hand out of my hair into it. I lean my head on his hand in mine and he cradles it. He sighs, then releasing my cinched fingers, he brings that hand to hold my head too. He tips my face down laying the same gentle, soft and firm kiss on my forehead. Leaving his lips on my skin, he stays to breathe. I rest my hands on his small waist and squeeze him. "You're welcome. I meant it." He draws back and looks at me as if he wants to say something else. I wait. I can see him trying to put the words together. He sighs. Looks away, then back. "You are so contagious." He takes a step back. The fresh air between us breaks the spell. "But we both have to go." He steps around me. I turn with him like a flower follows the sun unable to take my eyes off him. He smiles and winks at me. "Schiavo." At his truck, he reaches for the door handle and my eyes fall to his perfect, golden hand and I see it stopping the elevator again; I feel the power of his seduction; I hear him say, Aurelius and Siri, for the first time; I feel his kiss on my lips and my forehead. My heart starts to soar! *Life feels pretty fucking fantastic!*

"Ciao." He starts to climb in, relaxed, smiling that same beautiful smile he gave me the first time I laid eyes on him, but he stops, narrowing his eyes when he sees my mischievous twinkle. "What Wild Thang?" *I love my nickname.* "What are you thinking?"

I lean my head over, drop my eyes to the ground and let them travel up his physique like he did mine in the elevator, stopping at each point of interest, making him feel me. When I look into his face, he is still grinning and also has a mischievous twinkle. "We have unfinished business, Aurelius. A bottle of Merlot to open and enjoy, and rain-checks to cash."

"I can't wait to open and enjoy that deep, full body with its enticing flavor. And I've already been dreaming up ways to cash in on those rain-checks."

Walking away, I flip my hand in a wave. "See ya! Aurei."

I'm halfway to TD when I hear. "Hey Wright!" I stop and turn back to him. "Have a good time on your *not* hot date."

"Have a good time giving 'em hell at your farewell."

He laughs as I turn and strut my stuff to TD's car for him. *My ass isn't the only heart beating for you, Golden God! Umm. Umm. Umm.*

TD is pacing when I walk up. He doesn't recognize me until I say, "I'm ready. Let's go."

"Fuck Siri! You clean up good! But Goddammit, you're late. Get in. We have to go."

He opens the driver's side and gets in. I walk to the passenger side to open my own door. Knowing the Raptor is still there and that Aurei is watching me, I bend over at the waist keeping my legs straight and flash him a shadow glimpse of what lies between and beneath. As I slide in, I turn my face to look at him. He is sitting with the window down watching me. He whistles an old fashioned cat call, making me laugh. I give him a twinkling finger wave as I close the door. *I don't think either of us will hold out until Sunday. Tomorrow is the day.*

The car smells of smoke. "I didn't realize that was you with that guy. Who is he?" TD starts the car.

None of your business. I ignore his question. "I thought we were in a hurry. Let's go."

"We are." As he backs out, he looks at my tits and grins, but doesn't say anything. When we pull past Aurei, he is smiling and toots the horn a quick tap. My heart flutters.

Aurei pulls out behind us. He rides TD's ass down the drive and the truck headlights flood the car. I can feel the Alpha Male domination and I have to cover my smirk by looking out the window.

TD keeps checking the mirror, feeling the intimidation too. "What the hell does he want?"

Me! Which makes me grin, but I don't say anything. I continue to stare out the window while Aurei continues tailing us. When TD slows down to make a right turn, Aurei cruises past, hitting the horn three quick toots. *Tomorrow is definitely the day!*

I stare out my window not seeing anything, thinking instead about *Aurei. Aurelius Moore. That name suits him. Fuck yeah! Now I can check him out on FB!* I take my iPhone out of my purse, open my app and search 'Aurelius.' *He should be easy to find. And there he is!* I hit 'Add Friend,' then I send him a private message. "Here's my digits. 334-###-####. "Call Me Maybe." LOL! ;D" I hit send. I hum the tune as I see my reflection in the window. *That smile is Siri-ously crazy wild!*

TD starts to talk. "I'm a little uptight about tonight. I've been trying since I moved to bum-fuck

138

Alabama to get an invitation to this party. Do you mind if I smoke?"

"Yes, I do. Can you wait?"

"Sure. You look sexy as hell, by the way. I love the dress." He reaches over to touch my cleavage and I slap his hand away.

"No touching. That's Rule #1! Remember?" I state firmly.

"I thought you were just playing hard to get." He attempts to be charming and sexy.

"I am serious, TD. No touching. I'm not on a date with you. I thought I made that clear. I'm only attending this party because you were in a jam. Don't make me regret it."

"Or what?"

I lean up and over so he can see my face clearly in the lights from the dash board. "Listen Bubba, I can either make you the toast of the party tonight or I can ruin whatever chance you have of getting in … ever. Chew on that!" He cuts his eyes at me. "I don't give a shit what these people think of me, but you do. You need me."

"I understand what you're saying."

"Tell me. What's Rule #1?"

"No touching. Got it."

"Good. So, who's attending this late cocktail party?"

His phone rings. "Excuse me, I have to take this." He picks it up and answers it. "Rachael, you fucking bitch!" He laughs at something she says. "Are you back? ... No it's too late this time. Maybe next month ... I found a suitable replacement ... No, there wasn't time ... They'll get over it ... I wasn't waiting another month before getting to fuck her ... I'm so horny for her now I whack off in my damn office while I listen to them fuck ..." He laughs at what she says. "Yeah, my boner is back the minute I lay eyes on those giant tits .... If she wasn't a red head, I would have let it go, but I haven't fucked a red head yet, and those tits are downright fuckable themselves." He laughs again at something she says. "Hell yeah, I'm gonna fuck them too ... Yeah, yeah, I'll give you the low down tomorrow.... Sure... I'll call you when I get up." He ends the call, grinning and turns to look at me.

"So, I take it Mandy and Charlie will be here tonight?"

"Yeah, and you can bet your ass, I'm going to drool over her red tipped tits tonight."

"TMI, bro, TMI!" I roll my eyes. My iPhone FB notification dings. *So soon?* I snatch it up grinning. There are 2 red dots. I open it and sure enough, Aurei has accepted my friend request and answered my message. "Wild Thang! You are SO CONTAGIOUS!

Here's my digits, 334-###-####. There ain't no maybe!" I laugh out loud at that. I quickly enter Aurei's digits in my phone. First name: Aurelius. Last name: Moore of him! Company: Golden God!

"What's so funny?"

"Private joke." We ride in semi silence. I hum "So Contagious," and see the runway in Vegas. Seary opens the show with it. It's one of my favorites to dance to. The music is slow and allows for dramatic dance moves as I strip down to my G-string, teasing the men on the edges of the runway about how unexpected this is, falling in love at first sight with them. Then I pick one lucky one out, a birthday boy if I get wind of it ahead of time, and individually seduce him, saying he is the only one I will break it down with, giving him a shot and hanging on him. "So Contagious" is an all-time favorite of mine. *Crazy that Aurei would say that to me.*

TD slams on the breaks. "Damn, I almost missed it." There is a little dirt road just past the golf course entrance. He turns down it.

"Where is this cocktail party anyway?" The hair on the back of my neck stirs.

"It's down here behind the golf course another mile or two. It's super, secluded for privacy, but it's in a restored turn of the century plantation home."

"Well, that's cool! I thought of majoring in Architecture briefly."

"Really? You haven't always been a simple secretary then?"

Ha! If you only knew, who I really am. Your jaw would drop. "No. I haven't always been a simple secretary. My degree is actually in accounting."

"Really? I'm not sure which is worse a boring accountant or a simple minded secretary."

"Yeah, really!" I shudder.

We roll out of a sharp curve to see a row of trees planted to form a secure hedge. When he drives through the opening, my mouth drops open and I gasp. There in front of us is a beautiful, restored, 2 story, southern style, plantation home. Complete with columns on the full length front porch with a Cinderella style full length stairs leading to a circle drive, which is lit by carriage lamps. The yard is landscaped and manicured to perfection. *It is absolutely amazing.*

"WOW!" I say in complete awe.

"Wow!" TD says too. "Score a big one for the home team!"

TD parks the Porsche next to a BMW convertible which is parked next to a Mercedes Benz, which is parked next to a Jaguar, which is parked next to a Cadillac XTS. "Shall we?" He gets out, walks around the car and stands at the back.

I open my own door and walk to stand next to him. "This is spectacular! I had no idea this was here."

The house is fully lit, looking every bit the mansion it is. There is piped music from hidden speakers. As we walk to the porch, an uneasy feeling comes over me. "TD, are you sure of the time? It feels like we are crashing a party already in progress and we are very late."

"I'm positive. Why?"

"It's strange that there isn't any help or staff to greet us."

"Super secluded, private party means super secluded, private party."

On the porch, TD takes a cigarette out, lights it, and takes a heavy draw. He looks at me. Grinning, as smoke comes out of his mouth and nose. "I am going to have one hell of a time tonight." He leans his head back kinking the pony tail while he pulls another long draw. He laughs looking over the driveway. "And you are going to get the surprise of your life."

"Surprise? Of my life?"

"Yep." He exhales smoke straight up into the air.

I ball my fist up tight, push my middle knuckle out, and frog the fuck out of his arm, right on the point of his shoulder. *THUD!*

"SHIT!" He yells and drops his cigarette. "What the fuck did you do that for?" His arm hangs limp. Tears from the pain well up in his eyes.

"Here's an important fact about me. I don't take no shit from nobody, motherfucker."

His face visibly pales as he stares at the daggers in my eyes. "Just be cool. Don't go all ballistic on me now. You don't have to participate."

"You better pray I love the surprise of my life, you son of a bitch!" I say between clenched teeth.

He stares at me and a bead of sweat pops out on his forehead.

The alarm on his phone goes off. It's 10 sharp. The front door opens slowly. "Listen, Siri, before we go in. I'm sorry. Really. I should have told you what kind of party this is but you wouldn't have come. I only need you for the first part. After that, you can leave. Here's my key. Take the Porsche home." He hands me his key.

I slip it in my purse. *What the fuck kind of cocktail party is this?*

CHAPTER SEVEN

What I see when I enter the house leaves me speechless again. It's incredibly beautiful. There is not one but two spiral staircases on each side of the grand room with a huge chandler in the center. There is a balcony at the top with an elegantly carved banister that runs down both staircases. The landings at the bottoms are flared. *Dramatic and classy.* The entire floor appears to be black marble that reflects the chandelier. *This is really exquisite! Wow!*

My heels click as we walk in. The first thing I notice after taking in the house is that no one is breathing. Everyone has frozen right where they were when we walked through the door. *I'm used to making a dramatic entrance, but not one like this.* Shock and tension fill the air. *They obviously didn't know I was coming in place of Rachael.* I cut my eyes at TD. *He looks like a kid who got caught with his hand in a cookie jar in a candy store. Too excited to be really worried about the consequences.*

Standing in the center of the room between the staircases are four other couples. There are 3 men to my right in what appears to be a receiving line and their corresponding women are on the opposite side.

Darren Martin stands in the middle holding his wife Angela's hand. *They must be hosting the party.* I look at the men in line. I know each of them from my association at work. They are all friends of Mr. Connors.

Darren, who looks like Christian Bale, owns a chain of restaurants, nationwide. I don't know Angela but she must be a model from her looks and carriage. She reminds me of Marilyn Monroe. There is Mac Duckworth, who inherited a nationwide transportation company. I smile because Mac reminds me of Matthew McConaughey, and *who doesn't love Matthew?* He has on his Tony Lama cowboy boots and Stetson Hat with a tuxedo. Next is Brad Copper, who could be Matt Bomer's brother, very handsome and sophisticated. He inherited his money from his dad who sold Grapevine Communications for a fortune. Brad hasn't worked a day in his life. And last but not least, is Charlie Parks from work.

Darren turns to speak to Angela, who nods and walks over to the ladies where they huddle up, watching us and whispering. The men stand stock still, tense, staring at us as Darren walks over and speaks directly to TD. "Why isn't Rachael here?"

"She had a last minute emergency at work and had to cancel."

"You should have postponed this until next time. This is highly irregular."

TD's eyes dart to Mandy over Darren's shoulder. "I'm sorry. I brought Siri in hopes that she would be acceptable. I know y'all already know her and she is quite beautiful, isn't she?"

Darren looks at me. "Yes, you are quite beautiful. Forgive me for ignoring you. I don't mean to be rude, but this has never happened before. We have never allowed a surprise visitor to attend our swingers meeting."

My jaw almost drops open, but I hold it, putting on my poker face. However, I couldn't stop the blink of astonishment and the blood draining from my face. *Holy Fuck! Swingers! Shit!* Darren's eyes register my surprise but he continues as if he hasn't noticed. "I'm afraid you must sign a confidentiality agreement immediately. We will have to ask each person if they will accept you. It has to be unanimous. I'm sorry. If any one person doesn't approve, you will have to go home."

I nod. "I understand." I shoot TD a dart with my eyes. *God damn you, TD!*

He rubs the point of his arm and offers me a sly smile, knowing I'm not pleased about this surprise.

"Siri, please follow me. The form is simple. Nothing complex." Darren turns and walks away. I follow him while my mind whirls around the seriousness of my situation. *Swingers are all about fucking each other. It's one thing to be confident I can handle TD, but another to handle 4 more who all expect to fuck. Rule #1 is in serious jeopardy.*

Darren leads me under the balcony and down the hall to a small intimate office. When he closes the door, he asks me. "You did not know this was a swinger's party, did you?"

"No. I'm sorry. I didn't. TD invited me late yesterday afternoon to a cocktail party. He failed to tell me that it was an actual cock and tail sex party."

He frowns. "Siri, let me first apologize for TD's indiscretion. He isn't from around here, as you know. He doesn't understands the strict moral code we live under. If you are offended by our lifestyle choice, I apologize to you. You may leave after you sign the agreement. TD will take you home."

"Apology accepted. I'm not offended. I admire couples who have the honesty with each other to own up to their sexual preferences and who have the balls to openly fuck someone else under the same roof as their spouse."

His eyes widen, then he busts out laughing, relaxing.

"If the others find out I didn't know, that would jeopardize a very delicate bond of trust you have managed to maintain within your group. I get it. I'll stay and play."

"Great." He digs out a single sheet of paper and pushes it to me.

When I read it, I'm surprised at the simplicity. It simply states that everything that happens within these walls are held in complete confidence.

"Is this it? Is this the only rule?"

"Lord, no. We have unofficial Rules of Engagement for the playrooms upstairs, but this is the only legal document you are required to sign."

"I don't have problem signing this agreement." I pick up the pen, sign it and push it back to him, smiling.

He puts the paper away, stands, and surveys my breasts and my dress with appreciation. "Shall we join the others?"

"We shall." I question him as we walk back the reception area. "So, give me an idea, please, of what is in store. How do the couples hook-up? Do you play games?"

"First, we will make sure each individual member is ok with you joining. Then, we will go into the courtyard for some social foreplay. Everyone gets time with each other to dance and flirt. Tonight, because you are new, each man will make time for you. When the foreplay is over, we will go upstairs.

There are individual bedrooms for private fucking. In our house, we have given each woman her own room. You will get one too if you decide to become a permanent member."

"And, if I don't?" I ask.

"Then Rachael will be allowed to join TD. You can decorate the room in any manner you like. So far, the rooms reflect our women's preferred sexual tastes. There is, also, one big playroom where we play games. There is a nice entertainment system complete with a big screen TV where we've watched porn then had a group sex party. Everyone fucked everybody. It was wild!" He stops. We are standing around the corner. It's a short walk to the foyer where the others are waiting for us to join them.

"Do you ever hire professionals?"

He frowns looking puzzled. "Professionals? Do you mean prostitutes? No."

I laugh. "Professional entertainers."

"Oh, you mean strippers. No, but we recently installed a stripper pole and Angela is learning to pole dance."

"That's fantastic! Good for her! But I actually meant professional erotic entertainers and erotic dancers. You said you watch porn sometimes. Do you ever hire live erotic professionals to get your juices flowing?"

"No. Honestly, I never thought of that." He smiles and looks at my tits. "But damn! That's a fantastic idea! Do you know any?"

"I think I can help you out with that." I wink at him. "Shall we join the others now and get this cock and tail sex party started?"

He grins, offers his arm and I hook mine in it. Right before we enter the room, I joke with him. "I pray to Zeus, you know, because he is the Father of Fucking Gods, literally and figuratively."

He laughs out loud at that. "You are going to make a nice addition to our group." We walk back in, side by side.

Time to take control of this situation. I cross the room in full Diva mode in my Black & Blue Baby, clicking my heels on the floor, tits jiggling out the top, ass thumping like a heartbeat. I hear Aurei's long slow whistle. *Take control, protect Rule #1 and return to the Golden God unfucked. That's my goal.*

When I arrive in front of TD, I give him an 'I know something you don't know' look with a smile. *You are the one who is in for the surprise of their life. You have no idea who you brought, and what is about to happen, but it is going to be unforgettable!*

Darren announces that I have signed the contract and am willing to stay. He addresses the group in a formal way with a southern gentile voice and tone.

"We will now perform the proper introductions and vote on Siri." He addresses TD and I. "After the vote, if everyone agrees, the group moves to the courtyard to get acquainted before we move upstairs. We want you to relax and have fun! Everyone wins here."

Darren escorts me to the men in the receiving line while Angela takes TD and leads him to the women.

The first man is Mac Duckworth. "Mac would you like to welcome Siri into our house?"

I watch him as he assesses my assets. All men have a sexual tell, like a poker tell.

Mac takes off his Cowboy hat and nods to me. His eyes travel over my tits down to my pussy where they linger. I encourage him by parting my legs, and cocking my ass while I take my purse off my shoulder to hold as a clutch, putting my hand on my hip. The move causes my skirt to slide up my thigh as it is pulled taut. His eyes flare. *You're thinking, does she shave, wax, or leave her bush natural?*

He says in a country drawl. "Yes, I would *love* to welcome you, little lady."

When Darren and I step away, his eyes leave my crotch and finally find my eyes. *If you only knew, how special I treat mine, Cowboy!* I wink at him. He puts his hat back on and rolls a toothpick out of his mouth as he grins at me.

The next man is Brad Copper. "Brad, would you like to welcome Siri into our house?"

Brad's eyes stay on my face as Darren speaks and when he addresses me, they travel up and down my dress. "Siri, you look ravishing tonight, your style and grace are appreciated. Welcome." *Boredom. A man completely bored with sex. Poor thing. I'll relight your fire.*

We step to the last man in line, Charlie Parks from work. "Charlie, would you like to welcome Siri into our house?"

Charlie's eyes never find my eyes, my face, or my dress. They are glued to my tits. *A tits man, of course.* I can't resist the urge to tease him. I put my hands behind my back, holding my purse between them and squeeze my shoulder blades together. The fabric slides back as my tits push forward and the dress expands, exposing the edge of my nipples. His eyes not only flare, but he puts his hand to his lips and wipes them. "Absolutely. I vote yes."

"Me too." Darren says as he leads me to the middle of the room. I smile graciously at him.

Angela brings TD to join us where we swap escorts and sides. Angela takes my hand. "That is a killer dress you are wearing. You look sensational."

"Thank you."

She leads me to the beginning of the line and repeats the process with each woman. Most women don't have sexual tells to another woman, but they have other issues to deal with like jealousy, envy, bitches, mean girls, dominants, submissives. A whole host of emotional bullshit to try to figure out.

Mac's wife, Rosa is first. She stands under 5'5" tall. She has on bejeweled cowboy boots with a pants suit. Her posture says she's a rodeo queen. Her long hair is dark brown with light red highlights. She has it pushed behind her ears, the length falls wavy to the tops of her breasts. "Sure thang, honey, we are happy to have you." Her demeanor is open and warm. She is every bit a tom-boy. *I bet she likes to fuck as much as her husband does. No issues there.*

Brad's wife, Bella, is the natural beauty of the girls. Her pure black hair looks almost blue in the bright light of the chandelier and is cut short, but not cropped. Her complexion is creamy with flawless skin. Her face is angular but not harsh. She is in the 5'8" range. She is not skinny, but not curvy either. *She is an athlete, probably both golf and tennis.* Her eyes travel from my face to my tits and stay there. I see a sexual tell, and I test it to be sure. I put my hands behind my back like I did with Charlie and squeeze. My tits expand and her eyes flare ever so slightly. *Interesting.* She looks back up to my face.

"Of course, Siri, welcome." I let my smile spread slowly over my face and she responds with a sexy as hell smile that pings my gaydar off the chart. *Now, this is interesting. Bella is more complex than the others.*

Next is Mandy. Her long, straight, auburn hair is undeniably beautiful and her skin is pure like Bella's only rosy like Rosa's. Mandy smiles at me so sweetly, giggles, and hugs my neck. "I'm so happy you agreed to stay. I don't know how much longer TD could hold out." She winks at me and hooks my arm as we turn to look at TD. "He is threatening to fuck me by force if I don't give him some red haired pussy." He has reached Charlie, who slaps him on the back and they laugh about something or someone.

"You shouldn't have teased him so hard at work. Poor guy. He's had a hard on for you since his first day."

She laughs. "That's part of the game, girl! That's part of the fucking game."

Angela takes my hand to walk with me back to the middle of the room like little girl best friends sometimes do. She squeezes it. "Are you nervous? Excited? Scared?"

I answer truthfully. "Yes."

She whispers. "Relax, let your guard down and enjoy yourself. No one is going to hurt you here. The men love and spoil us. They will love you too." I look into her eyes. The depth of her sincerity stops me. "Sure, we are swingers, Siri, and we fuck each other for fun, but we are more than that. We support each other in all things. Darren and I will be your best friends, he will aim to please you in bed, and we will be here for you no matter what. Don't worry. The first time is always the hardest."

Her words touch a wound deep in my heart causing tears to come to my eyes. From the bullies that tortured me when I was little for having frizzy hair and big eyes, to the boys who pinned me in the locker room in middle school then took turns groping my DD tits, to the mean girls who shunned me after I won the high school beauty pageant, there hasn't been a handful of people who I count as sincere friends. There is Piper, Cat, Bart, and Brutus. No one from around here and no one from my childhood. She strokes my hair. "Love heals all wounds, Siri. This is a house of love." I squeeze her hand. She hooks my hand in the bend of her arm, pulls me toward Darren and says in a lighthearted, fun voice for everyone else to hear. "I do love the dress! Is it an original?"

"Yes, but it's a one of a kind, I'm afraid, made especially for me."

"It definitely looks like it was. It fits like a glove. I would love to have an evening dress made that would fit me that perfect."

"I would be happy to hook you up with my designer."

She smiles and raises her eyebrows making me laugh. "Ha! Not hook up like hook up, hook up like introduce you."

"I knew what you meant, I couldn't resist teasing you. It is exquisite and you look so beautiful in it."

"Thank you, Angela. That's awfully sweet of you to say."

"It's true," she says as Darren and TD join us. She takes the hand Darren offers her. "Follow us to the courtyard."

TD offers his arm and I take it. We leave the grand room foyer, going under the upstairs balcony, through one set of French doors into a horseshoe shaped veranda and out into the open air interior courtyard. The courtyard itself is not small but very intimate. It is beautifully decorated with patio willow trees, shrubs, and bouquets of flowers everywhere with the center clear for dancing and a full bar. There are only a few single chairs placed around the outskirts. I make my way to one, lay my purse down on the ground under it, and push it with my toe out of the way. *I don't want my gun to be discovered. That would surely give everyone cause for concern.*

I return to the perimeter of the dance floor while the others get their drinks at the bar. As I wait, I take in the view of the back of the immense house. It is amazing! The interior upstairs balcony joins the courtyard with twin staircases that run onto the roof of the verandah, then branch down to the courtyard and also continue below. There is hedge of shrubbery that forms the last wall breaking the view from the grounds behind the house. The sound of running water can be heard occasionally over the distant sound of the piped music and the chatter of the swingers. *The house is spectacular!*

The piped music goes quiet. Darren approaches me. "Angela requested a special song for our first dance." He bows. "May I have this dance, Siri?"

"I'll Be" by Edwin McCain starts to play.

I curtsey and accept his hand. "Certainly, Darren."

We waltz, very old school, very gentile, very rich, and very beautiful. As we whirl slowly and fully around the dance floor, the words to the song touch me again and I know I have found two more friends.

I see TD waltzing with Angela. *She is an excellent dancer. Perfect form, head held high, and face to the ceiling as they twirl. I am going to teach her to pole dance as my gift to the house.*

As the song ends, Darren pulls me into his embrace. I hug him totally relaxed. "I thoroughly enjoyed that! Thank you!"

He smiles. "Angela made a good choice then?"

"Yes, she did."

He escorts me off the dance floor to the bar as everyone else moves on to it to Pitbull's "Timber."

"What can I pour for you?"

"Crown, please. Neat."

He nods, pours it, and holds his in a salute as he hands it to me. "You are an excellent dancer, Siri."

We clink glasses.

"Thank you. Angela is too. Where did you find such a beautiful, elegant lady?"

He smiles. "She's 'My Fair Lady.'"

"So, you are Henry Higgins?"

"Yes." He smiles affectionately watching her.

"My congratulations to you both." I take a deep sip. The heat of the liquid feels good going down.

"You mentioned erotic dancers earlier. Do you know how to dance more … erotic?" He smiles over his glass searching my face. His demeanor is still southern gentleman, but there is a bad boy vibe.

"Yes, I do. What did you have in mind?"

"Something that will… how did you put it, get my juices flowing?" He grins with a wicked look in his eye.

"Def!" I grin back, matching his look. "I think that can be arranged."

"I'm going to be your greatest fan then."

"That spots already been taken, I'm afraid." I take another sip of Crown, and turn toward the others dancing, but I don't see them, instead I flash to the memory of my first customer.

He is sitting on a low chair in a private back room of the club. His hands are loosely bound behind him with his neck tie attached to the chair. *'Clay, what's rule #1?' I ask him. 'Rule #1: No touching,' he tells me. The music starts and I give him an erotic lap dance making him moan, over and over again, then he starts to swear, hating Rule #1. I tease him making sure he has gotten his money's worth, then Lei comes in to help with his happy ending. When she entered the room, she strutted up to him and said, "Clay, I don't have ANY rules." His eyes lit up. Before long she had him moaning to the rhythm of my dance, again and again, until he climaxed screaming my name."*

"There can be more than one, you know."

"Spoken like a true swinger." I hold my glass up to him, and we clink them.

"I hope you choose to fuck me tonight, Siri. I would love to be on the receiving end of your private, juicy, erotic dance."

I smile at him but don't say anything.

"I understand the night is still young and there are other choices, but keep me in mind. I love dance too. We have that in common." He takes my glass, sets it down and nods for me to look over my shoulder.

Mac saunters up as Joe Nichols, "Tequila Makes Her Clothes Fall Off," starts to play. "Siri, do you two step?"

"I do." He holds his hand out, I put mine in it, and he escorts me back onto the dance floor. I'm surprised at how 'smooth' a dancer he is. He guides me around the floor effortlessly. Managing to trot, pick our arms up and over, all without taking his eyes off my tits. He even spins me multiple times so the momentum makes them float freely in my open heart. When the song is over, he leads me back to the bar for another round of drinks and conversation.

"So, Siri, are you drinking Tequila tonight? I certainly hope so." He asks while eyeing my mons Venus. "Because I hope I get to see your clothes fall off."

"No. Sorry." He looks so disappointed it makes me laugh. "No, sorry; I'm not drinking Tequila." I clarify with a wink and he smiles. "I drink Crown Royal, neat." He pulls out the Crown bottle and pours my drink.

"But there's still hope I can see your clothes fall off."

I smirk. "Are you drinking Tequila? I hear it has the same effect on men."

He laughs. "I am! And it does!"

"Yee-haw!" I giggle at him. "Do you Rodeo, Mac?"

"Not anymore. I did when I was younger." He pours himself a shot of Patrón, licks his hand, pours salt, licks it off, slams the shot back and sucks the lime, all while smirking and watching me. *His tongue is long! I bet he knows how to lick a pussy!*

"Let me guess, you were a bull rider."

"No, I did timed events."

"Calf roping?"

"Yep. For the most part. I roped quite a few fillies too." He winks.

"I bet you did."

He laughs and pours himself another shot of Patrón. "I propose a toast to new and exciting … timed events."

As I hold my glass up to toast, I flash again to a memory. This time of a cowboy who wanted to pay to lasso me and tie me up like a calf in a Rodeo timed roping event, but when I told him Rule #1, he asked for another girl. Lei came in and replaced me. She joked to the other girls that he must have had a dark fetish desire to fuck one of his calves because he roped her, tied her up in 9 seconds flat and fucked her from the rear for a count of 30.

We touch our glasses. I take a small sip, but he slams his back, skipping both the salt and the lime this time. "That'll take the hair off!" He removes his hat showing me his premature balding head.

I crack up laughing. "You ain't right."

"I was, sure 'nough, hoping you would drink Tequila. Then I would have had an excuse to touch you off the dance floor before the party upstairs starts. We could have done body shots. You could have licked my head, put salt on it, and licked it again, while my face was buried in your beautiful boobs. Then, I could have put salt on your shoulder, licked it off, then drank my shot out of your cleavage. If only…."

I smirk. "You're a sly dawg."

"Yeah." He grins with only one side of his mouth and it is really sexy.

"But I'm drinking Crown." I look innocently at him.

"Damn shame too. I've got to quit looking at you. My stallion is so hard right now…." He turns away to watch the dance floor. "Damn shame!"

My eyes drift down to view the stallion's bulge. *Sweet Zeus, that looks like it belongs on Pegasus.* I turn to look at the dance floor too not wanting to think about fucking that.

"I can tell a Cowgirl when I see one."

"Yes, I used to be a Cowgirl. Growing up, my grandfather raised cows and I rode on his farm."

"Riding horses is a lot like fucking, don't you think?"

"Def!"

He chuckles. "Def, time to get you back in the saddle, babe. You could warm up by riding me later. I promise not to buck you off." He turns to face me, slides his hand down his cock once as he gives me that sexy sideways grin again. "I'm a sweet ride."

"I bet you are."

"I'm sure I could teach you a trick or two."

I laugh. *I'm sure I could teach you a trick or two too.*

He turns back to the bar, and pours himself another shot. "Here's to Cowgirls." He throws it back.

"Let There Be Cowgirls." *You're gonna get a special treat.*

164

Mac looks over my shoulder and nods, then excuses himself. I turn to find Brad standing behind me. He doesn't invite me to dance. He walks to the bar pours himself a glass of Lambrusco Italian Red wine. "Are you enjoying yourself so far, Siri?"

"Yes." I watch him over the rim of my glass as I take a sip of my Crown. *You are a very handsome man. Why are you bored?* He is studying me over the rim of his glass too.

I smile and he smiles. "Are you going to ask me to dance?"

"No, but you are *very* good. I enjoyed watching you."

"Thank you. *Do* you dance?"

"Yes." He drinks his wine, continuing to study me.

I sip my crown, letting him for a few minutes, then I break the silence. "The house is exquisitely beautiful."

"Ah, yes it is." He looks up at the balcony and the back of the house. He takes his time observing it, then his eyes fall back to me. "You are exquisitely beautiful too, Siri. You fit in nicely with us."

"Thank you." I respond automatically to his compliment.

He looks over at Bella who is standing next to Mandy while TD dances with Angela. She glances over to Brad and smiles at her husband. "Bella likes you very much. She thinks you have promise."

"Promise. Now that's an interesting choice of words, Brad." Bella turns her gaze to me and gives me her sexy smile. I nod at her in acknowledgement. Mandy leans in to whisper in her ear. Her enormous tits pushing into the side of Bella's tits. She turns her attention to Mandy, putting her arm around her, pulling her even closer. I smile knowing how that must really turn her on.

When I look back to Brad, he is smiling at me and I know that he knows that I know. "You aren't as innocent as you let on, are you?"

"You are a very astute observer, Brad Copper and I am too."

"Yes." He takes another sip of wine.

I turn to face him, giving him a direct, no bullshit stare. "We all have secrets, don't we? Some more than others, some we share with a select few and some we keep hidden."

He clears his throat uncomfortable by my directness.

I change the subject to put him at ease. "What is beyond the wall of shrubs? I hear water running."

"We have an infinity pool below. It looks out over the flower gardens."

"Sweet. How big are the flower gardens?"

"Five acres. The gardens surround the house and back up to the golf course. There is a path that runs along the west side connecting a fairway to the house."

"Interesting. What else will I find in the gardens besides flowers? Does it have any other use or is it only a flower garden."

He smiles relaxing, comfortable again. "We have hidden alcoves placed throughout the garden paths. We use them for private encounters in our monthly meetings."

"Why does a path connect the golf course to the house?"

"One of those secrets we keep hidden. Shall I share it with you?

"Please."

"Some members play outside the rules on occasion." He takes a sip on wine. "A golf game is used as a cover for a rendezvous with another member for an unscheduled encounter."

"Y'all try to find ways to spice it up?"

"Yes. Rules are important and necessary, but a little spice is nice too, you know."

"Otherwise, it gets boring."

"Exactly!"

"So, tell me about the spice. How many different combinations of spice, do you all use?"

"Pardon?" He frowns. "I'm not sure I understand the question."

"Let me rephrase it then." I look at Bella and Mandy watching TD. "Do the couples keep it girl on guy only, or is there a little diversity? Girl on girl?"

He shifts his stance slightly and doesn't answer.

"Not yet." I say for him. "But some would like too."

He nods and looks away to Bella.

I reach up and touch his arm. "Brad, you were right about me. I'm not as innocent as I let people believe. I have secrets too."

He looks back to me interested now.

"You haven't asked me any questions. Ask and I will answer them. Be bold."

He puts his lips together thinking. "Where do you dance?"

"Vegas."

He raises his eyebrows. *Now I have your attention.* "What kind of dancing do you do?"

"Erotic." I smile and wink.

His eyes survey my dress. "Can you be more specific on erotic?"

"I specialize in sexually suggestive seduction. I'm actually more of an erotic entertainer. I'm not just an erotic dancer. I like to call myself a sexologist."

"Now, that's interesting." He completely relaxes and smiles at me. "I think we both could use another drink."

"Yes. I believe we could." I watch him bartend. "I'm really happy Karma has opened this door for me, Brad. I really like y'all. I totally respect a person's choice to be completely honest with themselves and especially their spouses about the true nature of their individual sexuality. I admire it. It's courageous." He hands me my drink and pours his wine. "Have you heard the song 'Follow Your Arrow' by Kacey Musgraves? It's a cute little tune that pretty much sums up my philosophy. Fuck what others think, you can't please everyone, YOLO and all that cliché shit."

"No. I can't say that I have." He chuckles as he uses his wine glass to point to the flower garden. "Shall we visit the gardens for some privacy? I want to hear about dancing in Vegas."

"Sure."

I follow him down to the infinity pool. "Oh, my! This is unbelievably beautiful!"

"Let's enjoy the pool then. We can tour the gardens together another time."

I smile at his innuendo knowing he has accepted me now.

He spreads a towel out on the edge, rolls up his pants legs, then removes his shoes and socks. "Let's get comfortable, friend."

I slip mine off too, take his offered hand, and sit with him while we soak our feet. I start with graduation and tell him my whole story.

CHAPTER EIGHT

"That's quite a story." Brad says when I finish. "When are you going back?"

"I have a flight scheduled for May 1st."

"Why are you waiting till May? Didn't you quit your job here today?"

"Yes, I did. I had originally planned to return next week, but I met someone special." I sigh and kick my feet stirring the water. "It's hard to fall in love in my line of work. I get dubbed a whore immediately and every man so far can't get past that label. Which makes me realize how special a man will have to be to love me *and* want to share this life with me."

He puts his arm around me and gives me a hug.

I lean my head on his shoulder. "Meeting all of you tonight has really made me very hopeful that I can find an open, honest man too."

"I hope you find someone that will love and appreciate you too, Siri. Nothing's better than that. Bella and I are so fortunate to have found each other."

"Yeah, you really are."

He removes his arm and kicks his feet too. We sit there in silence thinking. I feel Aurei's eyes again as they pierced me the first time we connected, then the shock of how beautiful he is, then the passion my body had for him from the very first moment he touched me. *Damn. I sure hope he is the one.*

Brad starts to laugh out loud. It's contagious and I laugh with him. "What's so funny?"

"I had a ridiculous thought."

"What?"

"Lord, she isn't thinking that TD is the one?"

I bust out laughing at that. "Now, that's hilarious! Not that he isn't cute. He is. But he's not my type."

"No. You are too much woman for him."

"There you are." Bella says coming down the steps. We turn to look at her. I'm struck again by her grace and beauty. We stand up as she walks over to us. Brad holds his arm out and she slides into his embrace, puts a hand on his chest, kissing him sweetly on the cheek. "Charlie is looking for Siri."

"Thanks, baby. Siri has quite a story. I can't wait to tell you all about it tomorrow. It's really fascinating."

She smiles at me. "I can't wait to hear it."

Brad drops to his knees, takes the towel, and dries a foot for me, then puts on my shoe. *Totally*

Cinderella. I feel like a Princess. Bella puts her arm around me to steady me. I smile at her. "So, how did you two meet?"

Brad answers as he moves to my other foot. "We knew each other as children. She moved away. We lost touch. Both fell in love with the wrong people. Both experimented with sex." He repeats the process on his own feet. "Reconnected jumping out of a plane. Discovered we were both adrenaline junkies, fell in love and the rest is history."

Bella laughs. "That's the extremely short version."

I laugh with her, then ask straight forward. "How did you open up about being bisexual?"

Brad laughs and looks at Bella. "And there it is. Out in the open, honey. See how easy that was?"

"I'm sorry if I was too blunt. Forgive me." I put my hand on my chest.

Brad continues to look at Bella, but reassures me. "No, it's okay, but it's still a secret to the others."

I spit in my hand and offer it for him to shake. "It's safe with me until you're ready."

He laughs as he spits in his and shakes mine. "I'm ready to put it out there."

"What the hell, we're all equals in the house." Bella spits in her's too and we shake. "I'm still hesitating. The timing just hasn't been right."

"So, what special timing occurred for you to share with Brad? Did you just confess?"

"No." Bella laughs as she looks at him and he smirks at her. "He opened the door at a Halloween party and caught me in the act of getting my pussy licked by Wilma Flintstone and said, 'Excuse me, dear. Didn't mean to interrupt your little secret. Carry on.'"

Brad kisses her on the top of the head.

"Holy Fuck! That's awesome!" I crack up laughing with them, then I ask. "And … you became swingers why?"

Brad confesses. "I have a roving eye and can't resist other women. We thought the variety would help keep me contained."

"And has it?"

"Yes, so far."

Bella looks concerned at him. "But he is getting bored again." She turns to me. "Please consider choosing him tonight, Siri. You are very beautiful and I know he would like to fuck you but he won't ask directly. He likes the spontaneity."

Brad rolls his eyes. "Come on, let's get back, before Charlie comes down here looking for us."

I follow them back up the stairs to the courtyard. As soon as I step back into sight, Charlie makes a bee line to me. "Siri, I'm so glad you decided to come with TD. I've been wanting to fuck you since the day I first laid eyes on you. And Mandy has been bugging the shit out of me to get TD into the house."

I hook his arm. "Charlie! No small talk?"

He laughs. "No, doll. No time. We both know I've been fantasizing about you since day one. Those business suits didn't hide your beautiful assets." He says as he devours my tits with his eyes. "It's so rewarding to see them now displaced in such a dramatic fashion."

I laugh at him. *Wait till you see all of them. I know how to be dramatic!*

He leads me back to the bar. "We're about to start. Can I get you another drink before we head up?"

"No, I'm good, thanks."

Charlie says as TD joins us. "Keep in mind, Siri, when you make your choice tonight, I've been wanting to fuck you the longest."

"I promise to give you a night to remember."

He grins at TD, slapping him on the back as he walks to Mandy.

TD sidles up to me and I tell him looking at the group of Swingers. "You're one lucky, son of a bitch, TD. I don't appreciate the fucking swinger sex party surprise, and I'm going to punish you for that, but I like these people a lot. I've decided I'm going to make you the toast of the party after all."

"I knew you weren't as innocent as you portrayed yourself at work. You were never uptight about Charlie, Mandy and me. You just ignored us."

I cut my eyes at him. "That's very true."

"Do you know who you are going to pick to fuck tonight?"

"I'm not picking anyone."

He looks at me. "Mandy said earlier, you will get to pick first."

"I'm not picking anyone."

"You mean you are gonna fuck them all?" He looks shocked then smiles. "Damn! I will be the toast of the party."

I smirk and roll my eyes. "I almost forgot my purse. I'll be right back." I walk off to get my gun.

When I return, Darren taps his glass and formally announces to us. "It's time to move upstairs everyone." We follow Darren and Angela up the stairs without speaking.

"Welcome to the playroom. This is where all the fun starts."

TD proceeds in first, puts his hands in the air and spins around. "Wow! It's better than I dreamed it would be. This is fantastic!"

From the dark red carpeted floor to the matching dark red walls up to the ceiling which is black and gold leopard print with some red splashed throughout, *it is definitely a wow moment! Exotic, erotic, and classy.* White leather chairs, love seats, and couches surround the walls. Some are on elevated platforms. There is a huge flat screen TV on the right wall mounted high so everyone in the room can see it. Red and black closed cabinets line the entire wall with painted naked silhouettes of men and women and couples engaging in various sexual positions. The room is equipped with surround sound and the soft romantic music from the driveway is playing in here too.

As I scan the room, I notice several things immediately that get my attention. *Cameras mounted in the corners, tracking spotlights, and the stripper pole is on a proper platform. Good.* I walk straight to it at the other end of the room.

TD is right behind me. "Wow! They have one of these. Who do you think dances on the pole?" He doesn't wait to hear my answer. "I hope it's Angela. She's beautiful. I prefer blonde's but Mandy is the target tonight."

Bella comes to me. "Siri, we store our personal items in the cabinets. Here let me take yours for you. I'll put it in the cabinet next to the door."

I hesitate knowing my Ruger is in it and she will be able to tell by the weight. "That's ok. I'll put it up. Where?" We walk back up to the cabinets and she shows me my space. I ask as I set it down. "What else do these cabinets hold?"

"Some of our sex toys."

"Cool, can I see what all you have?"

"Later. Right now, Darren is about to review the rules."

I walk back to TD by the stripper pole as Darren closes the door and comes to the middle of the room to address us. "Welcome again to Siri and TD. You are about to be inducted into our exclusive, private swingers group. We are a Ken and Barbie association. No one is allowed in who has kids and are over the age of 35. If you are ready, we will begin with the Rules of Engagement."

I smile warmly at everyone. "Yes. Let the games begin."

TD rubs his hands together. "Hell yeah, I'm ready to fuck."

Charlie chuckles. "Hell yeah, me too."

Darren starts. "Very well, Rule #1: We do not talk about our group. Rule #2: We DO NOT talk about our group."

Modified Fight Club rules?

"Rule #3: If someone says, 'stop' or goes limp, or taps out, the sex act is over." Rosa shifts her feet and Mac smiles at her.

We have a couple of BDSM fans amongst us. Ok. I can work with that.

"Rule #4: Sexual contact with non-members is strictly prohibited." Mandy runs her finger down her cleavage and then puts it in her mouth, rolling her tongue around it as her eyes find TD's. I know without looking that TD has a boner. "Rule #5: A new member each meeting will start the drawing from the hat. No consecutive repeats are allowed. The last member gets to determine the type of hook ups for that meeting." He clarifies for me and TD. "Independent, or group. Private or public. Game or entertainment." TD frowns. "Let me give you an example. For instance, last month Angela went first. She drew Brad, but had to pick again because she hooked up with him last time. The next pick was Mac. Brad ended up being last so he got to decide what everyone was doing. He choose strip poker with erotic dice. We played until everyone was naked, then we fucked the partner we had been assigned, but there was a lot of sucking and licking beforehand. It was a lot of fun, wasn't it?" The others nod and agree.

"Sounds like a great way to keep it fresh."

"Rule #6: No sex is allowed outside of these walls except with your partner and no sex with your partner is allowed inside these walls."

TD blurts out. "What the …? Wait a minute."

Darren stops and looks at him. "Do you have a question?"

"What's up with all these rules?"

"We are a swingers group, TD. We fuck for fun. We work hard not to get emotionally attracted to each other. Attached, yes, but not attracted. The Rules help define that."

"Yeah, yeah, yeah, I get that, but you mean to tell me that even though I'm in the group now, I can't fuck these beautiful ladies outside the house, anytime we want?"

"Yes, that's exactly what I'm saying. Only in here, only once a month and only one a month. If we allowed fucking each other anytime outside the walls without the rules, it would essentially be having an affair, and none of us want to jeopardize our marriages for sex, but none of us wishes to be monogamous either." TD looks agitated and eyes Mandy frowning. "TD, when we first began, I went 8 months before I fucked Rosa. Bella and Mandy swapped me and Mac back and forth while Angela and Rosa swapped with Charlie and Brad." He looks at his friends. "I was starting to feel like I had three wives." Everyone laughs. He looks back at TD and me. "It's harder to understand without being in the constraint of a marriage, but these rules have really been a blessing. It's too late now. You can't back out."

"No, no, I don't want to back out. I'm good. I need to fuck!"

Everyone laughs. Darren reassures him. "That's what it's all about."

"But just to clarify, I can't fuck anyone outside these walls but my partner?"

Darren looks from TD to me. "That's how the rules are written."

TD frowns and looks at the floor, then back up to Darren. "Since Siri and I don't fuck, what about Rachael? Can I at least continue to fuck her?"

Darren freezes. "I thought … wait a minute. Didn't you tell us …. Are you saying you FUCK YOUR SISTER?" He blurts out shocked.

What? For the love of Zeus! What the fuck?

"Yes." TD answers without hesitation.

Everyone is shocked and looking at him with their mouths open. He looks around, sees their faces and quickly recovers. "She's not blood!"

"Who is she then?"

"She was my step sister. My mother married her father when we were 15. They lasted about 6 months, but Rachael and I have been hooking up ever since. It's not incest!"

Angela puts her hand on her heart. "Oh, thank god!"

TD rephrases his question. "My question is since I fuck Rachael and she was supposed to come, and I don't fuck Siri, can I at least continue to fuck Rachael?"

Darren answers. "I think that will be alright. Any objections?" No one objects. Everyone nods. *They are too relieved Rachel isn't his real sister to object.* Taking a deep breath, Darren continues with the rules. "Rule #7: No lube, no condoms, no hard on, no problem." He points to the cabinets under the TV behind him. "Siri and TD, you will find plenty of different varieties in there. Help yourselves. Rule #8: All forms of sex are allowed as long as the parties involved agreed before starting. All parties achieve orgasm. Everyone leaves here happy and sexually satisfied."

Relaxing with this news, TD grins. "That's what I'm talking about."

"Rule #9: If this is your first night with a new partner, you HAVE to fuck." TD fucks air making everyone laugh. He is back to being the charmer. "And Rule #10, which we use only on the night of initiation of new members, if it applies, and I believe it will. If the woman is a virgin to the swinger's lifestyle, she is allowed to make additional Rules of Engagement for tonight only."

"Why?" TD wants to know.

"This is a little token of our desire to help her feel comfortable and in control while she gets her feet wet fucking someone other than her partner."

"Why only the woman?"

"Because women are generally less comfortable hooking up with different partners, particularly if they haven't chosen him. They are more discriminate than men." He looks with sincerity at me. "We want everyone to be comfortable, leave sexually satisfied and know they are in control." TD nods. "We strive to make sure our women are treated as equals."

All eyes are on me. "Siri, is this your first time as a swinger? Are you a virgin?"

I smile at each person starting with Darren, then Angela, Brad, Bella, Mandy, Charlie, Mac and Rosa. Each one is smiling at me. Charlie is leering, but that's just Charlie. My heart warms to them. *I'm going to give you all a show you will never forget! It's what I do and I'm damn sure good at it! It is going to be epic! I love what I do! And you will all love it and me!*

"Yes, Darren, I am." I answer truthfully.

"Then, you have the floor. What rules would you like to implement to make you comfortable?"

"Let me see." I say as I walk up to the stripper pole. With my back to them, I put my hand on it, run my open fingers from the bottom to the top. My hand slides smoothly. I cock my ass, release my hair from my comb, and drop it on the floor as I shake my hair out. I look over my shoulder at them. "You aren't the only ones who have a secret life." I bend at the waist, dip my shoulder toward them and give them a classic stripper's roll up, complete with a full hair flip. "Everyone has secrets." Lifting my right foot off the floor, I place it on the pole and slide my foot up doing a split on it. I look out at them. "Some of us are better than others at hiding them."

Everyone has stopped breathing, stunned.

I slide my foot down until I can hook the pole with my knee, then I clinch it and pull my body to the pole, mounting it, scooting twice to the top. *Good. It's firm. No wobble.* Next I straddle the pole with straight legs in a scissor grip as I rotate my body 90 degrees to a position horizontal to the floor. Holding the pole with my top hand, I point to my audience. "Tonight is going to be a night you will never forget." I pull my body back to the pole in a sitting position with my legs still straight out. Grasping it with both hands, I swing my legs down for momentum, arching my back, pushing my body away then I swing both legs on the same side of the pole, up and over my head. I push off at the peak and flip upside down, doing a pole hand stand. I hold that position, pausing for effect.

No one has made a sound. All eyes are on me.

I open my legs in a full straddle split and pivot my body out away from the pole, then I slowly do a controlled rotation around the pole. *Yes. I'm a professional pole dancer.*

They are in complete shock.

Hooking the pole again with my top leg at the knee, I dangle my body and continue the slow rotation down. When my hands are almost to the floor, I grasp the pole, release my knee, lower one leg until it touches down, then I drop the other one and stand. My feet are shoulder width apart and my back is to my captivated crowd. I look over my shoulder at them with my head tipped down. My hair fans my shoulders. I drop my ass all the way to the floor and clap my hands when it touches then push back up to stand with my head tipped back and my face to the ceiling. The sound makes them take a collective breath and the quick move makes my skirt hike up on my ass, showing my cheeks hanging out. I poke my ass toward them and shake it.

Mac gives a sharp whistle.

Time to make them fans for life. I mount the pole again. Climbing up to the top, I prepare to do a move I learned from <u>Jenyne Butterfly</u>. It is Surreal's signature move. From an upright position, I grip the bar between my calves, and in one swift motion with perfect timing and angle, I push off the pole letting go completely with my arms over my head, mimicking a backward dive. As my body drops, my legs pivot on the bar. My knee hooks the pole, as my other leg drops, providing a counter weight, catching and stopping me.

There is a loud collective gasp and the women squeal.

I hang there for only a second before I clasp my free leg. I pull it to my face doing a cocoon move while I push my tits against the open heart in my dress. Gravity, position and pressure plunge my beautiful big breasts out into the open heart allowing them to burst free and bounce on the heavy sequined trim. They are on full display. I smile knowing, *no one is immune to that.*

Mac cusses with a real southern drawl. "Gawd daaaamn!"

Darren exclaims. "Jesus H. Fucking Christ!"

Charlie blurts. "Holy Fucking Hell!"

Even Brad comments. "Sah-weeeeet!" *Nothing boring about this!*

186

I rotate down the pole, one complete turn, then I put my legs together, hook the pole in my elbow, and brace against it with the other hand. I pivot using my arms and body against the pole, doing a split until my foot touches the floor. When my stiletto is solid, I close the split and stand up. With my back to my audience, I bend over at the waist, poke my ass at them, and jiggle my cheeks as my tits slide back securely into the bodice. *My Black & Blue Baby is truly a fucking work of art.* I swing around the pole to face them. "I have secrets too."

"Obviously!" TD blurts out.

"I'm a professional erotic entertainer." I lean my chest on the pole putting it between my tits. I titty fuck the pole with deep, long, slow strokes as I speak. "My job is to stimulate your senses until you are ready, willing and begging for orgasm."

No one is breathing.

"Here are *my* rules." I slide slowly down spreading my legs letting the pole block their view. When I'm sitting on my high heels, I lean to the right. "Rule #1: No touching me." I hunch the pole, deep and slow, then lean to the left. "Rule #2: No touching each other until I say GO." I hunch the pole again, deep and slow.

Darren drops Angela's hand. She takes a step away.

I lean to the right. "Rule #3: No touching yourself unless I say so."

Charlie takes his hands out of his pockets, grinning.

I rise and step to the left. "Rule #4: You may only say four phrases." I bend over and twerk. "Go, Baby, Go." Then I step to the right, bend over and twerk. "Faster, bitch, faster." I stand up, walk around to the front, turn my back to them, straddle the pole with my feet shoulder width apart, and look over my right shoulder. "Fuck me!" I grab the pole with both hands, drop down to my ankles, bouncing at the bottom three times while my arms stay stiff, hand fucking the pole. Then I repeat looking over my left shoulder, bouncing, jacking the pole off. "Fuck yeah!"

Standing back up, I turn to face them and walk to the edge of the platform. I blow a few stray strands of hair out of my face, wipe my hand across my brow and smile at them. "Rule #5: With every orgasm, you will say, scream, or shout Seary, that's S. E. A. R. Y." I put my hands on my hips and say, "Any questions so far?"

Darren and Angela answer correctly. "Fuck me!"

Brad is silent, but Bella says, "Fuck yeah!" She turns to high five him and he smiles at her, slapping her hand in the air.

Rosa claps and Mac tells me. "Go, Baby, Go!"

Charlie and Mandy laugh and say together with TD. "Faster, Bitch, Faster!"

"Rule #6: We will play Gorilla at the end of the night. Everyone plays. No exceptions. I'll explain those rules when we play, but here's the twist. The last one to orgasm wins and he, or she, will shout GORILLA! The first one to orgasm loses and they forfeit their right to pick partners for the next full year!"

TD blurts out. "Fuck that!"

I turn my attention on him and raise one eyebrow while I wag my finger. "Not one of the choices. Which brings me to Rule #7: If you break the rules, you will be spanked."

Rosa gives us a "Fuck yeeeeah!" Everyone laughs. Everyone but TD.

I walk to stand behind the pole putting my back to the swingers again. Reaching up over my head with both hands, I grab the pole, then arch my back pushing the cheeks of my ass against the metal. I bend my knees slightly and my skirt slides up and off my ass, leaving my butt cheeks hugging the pole like my tits earlier. I turn my head to the right side and tell them. "When you leave tonight, I promise each of you, that you will never forget what happened here." I squeeze my cheeks together and the pole

189

almost disappears. I look to the left side. "I promise each of you, that you will never forget me." I squeeze my ass again then let go of the pole and wiggle my hips till my skirt drops back down over my booty. No one moves. All eyes are still on me. I walk to the edge of the platform, point at TD then motion him to come to stand beside me. When he is next to me, I ask him. "TD, I will need someone to help me. As my partner here tonight, you don't mind, do you?"

"No, I would be happy to help." He gives the swingers a thumbs up.

I laugh and wag my finger at him again. "Not one of the choices."

He looks surprised, then caught. He rolls his eyes and puts his hands up covering his chest and backs away playing the charming misunderstood douche card like he did in the office on Thursday.

I square my shoulders, follow him and poke my finger in his chest as I command. "No excuses. You were warned. You are gonna get a spanking."

He puffs his lips blowing air out and gives me a look that clearly says, 'no fucking way am I submitting to a spanking,' then he tries to bluff me with a confident smirk.

I cock my eyebrows at him with a more confident smirk of my own. "Down here in the South, TD, we spank that ass when boys are bad." I look to the others. "Ain't that right? What say y'all? Rules are rules! Right?"

Darren agrees. "Go, baby, go!"

Rosa chimes in. "Faster, bitch, faster."

Bella gives me a "Fuck me!"

But when Mandy says "Fuck yeah," he knows it *is* going to happen. The blood drains from his face then resignation settles over it.

I walk to the edge of the platform and wink at Rosa. "I bet you have a riding crop around here somewhere. May I borrow it?"

She giggles. "Fuck yeah!" Then runs to get it.

I walk back to TD and command. "Bend over." He bends over offering his ass to me. I step down off the platform and walk around to TD's face. I speak to him, but address the others. "So, TD, let's answer a few questions while we wait for Rosa. Did you omit the fact when you invited me that this cocktail party tonight was a swinger's cock and tail sex party?"

"Fuck yeah." He says quietly.

"And didn't you laugh when you told me that I was going to be in for the surprise of my life?"

"Fuck yeah." He admits to them.

"And didn't I explain clearly to you that I don't like surprises."

"Fuck yeah." He acknowledges.

"And didn't I explain clearly to you that I don't take no shit from nobody?" I lay my hand on the point of his shoulder where I frogged him on the porch.

"Fuck yeah."

"Good." I reach up and squeeze his wounded shoulder hard. He flinches. "So, when I say that you will do whatever I want tonight as part of your punishment, you agree that that's fair?"

"Fuck yeah."

Rosa comes back in with a jockey riding crop. "Good. Just so we are clear on that." Rosa walks up to me a little out of breath, and hands it over with a wicked smile on her face. "Thank you, dear." I take it from her and examine it. "This is nice, Rosa. The tress is wide and flexible." I test it on my palm. It makes a sharp cracking sound, but the sting is minimal. "It will do very nicely." I hit my calf hard and the cracking sound makes TD flinch. A red welt rises immediately so I show it to him. *I bet you've never had a spanking before. I bet your Mother used time outs instead. That's why you are so spoiled. Well, it's time you learned about spankings.* I step on the platform, walk around to TD's ear and whisper to him. "You are actually getting this spanking because one, you didn't tell them you were bringing me; two, you didn't obey their rules; and three, you were

192

flippant about how they would feel about it." I squat down in front of him so we can look into each other's eyes. "These are good people, TD. You don't deserve to be here." He blinks, and looks down. "Look at me." He looks back up into my eyes and I see real remorse. "You have to earn your right to be a member now. Do you understand?"

He nods. "Fuck yeah."

"Ok, get your attitude right. I'm going to give you an opportunity to redeem yourself." I stand, speak to him but address the others again. "TD, would you like Mandy to do the honors of spanking your ass?"

"Go, baby, go."

"Now, we are learning." I laugh, patting the top of his head with the crop. "Good boy." There are chuckles from the others. "Mandy, would you like to spank TD's ass?"

She looks at Rosa who tells her. "Go, Baby, Go."

She looks at TD's ass and says as she nods. "Fuck yeah."

I lean over and wink at him. "She's in." The others chuckle again. "Come on then. Join us." She flitters and bounces to the stage. "Stand here." I point to a place at his front. She stands there waiting for further instructions grinning at Charlie and the others. "TD, kneel before Mandy." He drops to his knees and looks up at those giant tits towering over him. "Mandy, Go. You may touch him. Start with his face." She looks surprised, but leans over, reaches out with both hands and caresses his cheeks and temples. He visibly relaxes with her touch. "Ah, how sweet." She grins at me. "Would you please undo his French braid? It's distracting." The others chuckle again. Mandy reaches around both sides of his head to remove the pony tail band then she runs her fingers through his hair letting his long locks hang free.

His face is inches from her tittys. He says "Fuck yeah" as a moan.

She giggles as she pulls his hair forward to his face. "Now, TD, please stand up." He does so but his eyes never leave her tits. "Mandy, remove his shirt." She cuts her eyes to the riding crop and I see a trace of fear in them. "Don't worry. You aren't going to flog him." I turn to the onlookers. "But we aren't going to spank a fully clothed person now, are we?"

Charlie answers with "Go, Baby, Go!"

Mandy starts at the top unbuttoning his collar first. His eyes stay glued to her tits. After each button, she gives him a variety of facial turn ons, a lick of her lips, an "O," a tongue flick across her teeth. *She is good at the teasing game.* When she has undone the last button, she turns to look at me for further instructions, keeping her hands on the top of his jeans.

"Pull the shirt out. We will leave his pants on … for now." Turned on by her own teasing, she doesn't simply pull the fabric out, she reaches in his pants to get it. Her hand rubs his dick on the way down making him close his eyes. *Wow! She is really a fantastic tease.*

Everyone is quiet. Their sexual tension starts to fill the room.

As she slides her hand out with the shirt, she strokes his erection. His moan of "Fuuuuuuck meeeeee" is full of pent up passion. *Let's see how serious a tease she is.*

"Mandy, now skin please."

She grins wickedly at me. *You know what I mean.* She asks permission. "Go, baby, go?"

I nod. "Yes, you may."

She turns her wicked grin to TD as she pulls her top down off her breasts. They fall out into the air, uninhibited. *Her nipples are hard, but they are always hard.* TD groans like a growl. She smiles feeling her power. *You get a gold star.* Their eyes lock. *There goes the world, falling away.*

"Well, that's certainly beautiful skin, but his skin, dear. Show us his skin." She lays her hands on his stomach and slides them up his chest and down over his shoulders, pushing his shirt off as her nipples touch and rub him. His shirt falls but hangs on his arms. She has forgotten to undo the buttons on his wrist. His eyes stay glued to hers as he holds one wrist up for her. *He is lost in her. Oblivious to us now.*

"Go, baby, go?" She asks for him.

"Yes, he may go, baby, go." I give permission.

She lays his hand on her tit cupping her breast. As she undoes the button, he flicks his thumb across her nipple. She moans to him. "Fuck me!" He offers the other wrist and they perform the same sensual unbuttoning. Before he takes his hands away, he squeezes them together, watching her already deep cleavage become a fucking gorge. *I know what he is visualizing. He is picturing his penis moving up and down, fucking them.* I let him tease himself with his thoughts, then I lay the crop across her tits. He releases them and takes a small step back. His eyes look tortured. The shirt falls softly to the ground.

"Mandy, please grab the hair on each side of TD's face and pull him down to resume the spanking position." She reaches up, wraps her fingers in his hair and pulls his face into her cleavage. He buries his face, nuzzling them, as he bends over at the waist. She releases his hair, and strokes his head, giggling at all the attention he is giving them.

I place the crop on Mandy's breast bone and push her back so his face is free of her tits. "We don't want him to suffocate." She giggles again. *Time to teach you how to dominate a man, baby girl. I think you're gonna like it.* "Mandy, stand here, in front of me." I hold the crop out to her. "You are giving the spanking. You will decide how hard and how many, but I will tell you when. Do you understand?"

"Fuck yeah."

"Good. Take the crop, turn around to face TD and repeat after me." Mandy takes the crop from me, weighs it in her hands, and smiles. Then she turns around and faces TD. I step up within inches of her body so she can feel my presence. I tell her what to say and she repeats me. "TD, kneel before me."

"TD, kneel before me." He drops to his knees.

"Bow your head to me." He bows his head.

"Repeat after me." He listens.

"You are a bad boy." "You are a very bad boy." "You deserve this punishment." "You want this punishment." "You need this punishment." "You will obey my every command." "You are my submissive. I have complete control over you." "You will answer me with 'Fuck me Madam.'"

"Take your belt off."

"Fuck me Madam."

"Unbutton your pants."

"Fuck me Madam."

"Slide your zipper down." "Pull your cock out. Let me see it." "Push your pants off that ass that needs to burn." "Hold your cock up for me. I need to see if you will satisfy me."

"Mandy, stand over him and examine it. Then spit on it and tell him to stroke it until it is good and hard for you, but don't let him whack off. Give him only a few strokes. Tease him. Touch your own tits while he does this. Get him going."

She smiles and takes a step up to him to tower over him. She takes the crop and puts it on his bowed face and pulls it up. "Lean back. I want to examine your cock!" He leans back on his heels holding his semi-soft dick in one hand and bracing with the other. Putting her hands on her hips she leans over to see. "That's not good enough." She stands and drops a well-aimed drooling spit out of her mouth onto the end of his penis. "Stroke it for me." He lubes it with her spit and it gets hard. "I like it faster, bitch, faster." She spits on it again. He rev's it up. It is rock hard now. "Stop. Let me look." Leaning over so her tits swing toward his face, she tell him. "Not bad, but you need to be harder to satisfy me." She straddles him, showing him her beautiful tits. She runs her fingers around the nipples. They shrink up tight and elongate, then she pinches them. His dick responds.

It starts to turn deep red. She tells him. "That's better." She spits on him again. "Stroke it slow, squeeze it hard. My pussy is young and tight." He does as he is told while his eyes devour her tits. She looks from his cock to his face and sees his look. "You like these, don't you?"

"Fuck me Madam."

She pulls one to her mouth and flicks her tongue on it. The audience breaks their silence offering encouragement with my phrases as everyone gets turned on. "Go, Baby, Go. Faster, Bitch, Faster. Fuck yeah. Fuck me!"

"I like them too." And she sucks her own nipples.

"Fuck me Madam."

I can see that they are both heading down the path of no return, so I step up and say behind her. "Stop stroking." She repeats me. He stops and when he releases his grip, his penis pulsates, throbbing. We wait until his throbbing has stopped. "Ok. He's ready again. I want you to feel the power of the crop now. Talk dirty to him as you stroke him with it." She takes the crop to his penis. She runs it up and down, tapping the tip gently. "I want to tap your cock, TD."

It responds immediately getting hard again. "Fuck me Madam."

"I want to tap it on the tip." She taps him with it. "I want to tap it at the base." She taps him. "I want to tap it up and down and up and down." She strokes him in little tapping motions. "You want to tap my pussy tonight?"

"Fuck me Madam."

"I want you to FUCK my pussy tonight."

"Fuck me Madam." His cock is rock hard again.

"What?" She barks. "What did you say?"

"Fuck me Madam."

"Fuck who?" He hesitates. She moves to stand in front of him, towering over him, bending over and leaning her tits to his face. She commands him. "Suck my tit." He opens his mouth and she sticks one in. The whole room moans. She pulls away and asks him. "Who's getting fucked tonight?"

"Fuck me Madam." His penis is red and swollen.

"No." She dangles the crop on the end of his penis. As she speaks, the end of the crop gently swings to touch his tip. "You will FUCK ME! Hard. Fast. Slow. Pounding my pussy. Over and over again until I scream. Do you understand? WHO ARE YOU FUCKING?"

"You. Madam. FUCK YOU MADAM!" He shouts back at her.

She laughs. "Oh dear, TD. That's not allowed. Time to be spanked." She backs away and looks to me.

I smile approvingly at her. "Very good. You learn quick. Strip him."

"TD, strip!"

"Fuck me Madam." He rolls on his back, pulls his shoes, socks and pants off. Tossing them to the side where his shirt is. His cock is purple and throbbing as he gets to his feet.

There isn't a soft dick or a dry pussy in the room.

Mandy commands him with authority. "Bend over." He bends over at the waist placing his hands on his knees. She walks around him, examining him. "Bow your head."

He hangs it. "Fuck me Madam." His hair falls on either side of his face, blocking his view.

At his ass, she lines up getting ready to do the deed. I whisper to her. "Don't forget. You decide how hard and how many." She nods. "Stroke the crop." She puts her hand on it and slides her hand up and down it, feeling the leather binding tickle her palms and her fingers. Her excitement is brewing. "Stroke it faster, bitch, faster." She hand fucks it. Her eyes shining. "Now. Punish him." I tell her.

She brings the crop back and … I catch it at its peak, holding it there, forcing her to submit to me.

She releases it and I take it from her. Stepping between her and TD, I wait until her eyes are locked on me instead of TD's ass. Then I run the leather over her taut nipples. They respond instantly, getting harder and longer. She looks down at them to watch. Flicking my wrist, I pop the crop twice, laying a well-aimed direct hit with precisely the right amount of force, on each taut tit. She squints from the pain and gasps.

Angela and Bella jerk and gasp too. Rosa, however, sucks her breath through her teeth. "Fuck me!"

Mandy's breathing quickens. Her eyes glaze. She stands there, speechless. I drag the crop again over each one. She pushes them out as she bites her lip. I pop them both again and she quivers. Her breathing changes to panting. She watches me with hunger in her eyes.

I hold Mandy's gaze and say loud enough for everyone to hear. "Rule #8: If you don't apply the discipline appropriately, you will be disciplined."

Rosa lets out another excited "Fuck me!"

I step up to Mandy so that our tits touch. When I lean over to whisper in her ear, my bodice rubs her nipples making her hold her breath. I lay the crop on her neck and drag the binding down as I whisper in her ear. "But you will find that discipline can be pleasurable." I blow in her ear and down her neck following the path of the crop as I back away. Stepping back, releasing the pressure from my presence, I take the crop and roll the tress lightly around each point of each nipple then push down roughly so it springs back into place. She closes her eyes. Again, I drag it gently teasing them. Her legs are quivering. When she opens her eyes, she gives me a piercing look. I hand the crop to her again and back away. She eyes it with new understanding. I wink. "Mandy, please apply the appropriate discipline to TD's ass. Remember he is a bad boy." She pulls the crop back, pauses at the top then swings it forward, but right before impact, she hesitates. It smacks his right butt cheek with little velocity, but his body flinches and his ass clenches nevertheless. She stares at his ass for a few moments. "Try again. That didn't satisfy *you* at all."

Not taking her eyes from his ass, she walks to the other side and pulls the crop back needing to see his reaction. This time she swings with more force, and right at the end, she flicks her wrist. The crop smacks his skin with a crack. His ass constricts, hunching. Her eyes get shiny again. Her breathing excited, panting.

"Now you're feeling it."

She looks at me with both appreciation and anticipation. She boldly steps to TD's face and commands him to "Suck my tit!" He latches on and sucks her hard and fast. She moans. "Stroke your cock for me." He drops to his knees and kneels. She spits on it. He strokes it falling forward onto his hand offering his ass again. She walks behind him and commands him. "Faster, bitch, faster!" He is whacking himself off as she returns to punish his right butt cheek. This time when she rears back, she knows she needs to feel it. She needs to feel his pain to give her pleasure.

With one smooth, fluid back stroke, she delivers a blow so fierce and firm that it takes him by surprise. The crack resonates around the room. "FUCK.... ME.... MADAM!" He shouts as he climaxes, shooting his semen.

There is dead silence in the room.

Mandy stares at TD on all fours with two red whelps on his ass, his head hanging down, breathing through the pain and pleasure of his orgasm. Smiling, I think how beautiful she is with her luscious auburn hair tousled from her swing as she closes her eyes, leans her head back and shakes her whole body releasing the passion.

"Go, Baby, Go!" Charlie says as he watches his wife have her first 'orgasm' without fucking.

When Mandy opens her eyes, she looks directly into mine. "Seary."

I smile gently at her. She smiles, wickedly back. I lower my voice again and say only to her. "Have him put his underwear on, then take the rest of his clothes to the cabinet, please. He isn't going to be needing them until he leaves tonight." She hands the crop back to me, stands over him, dominating, and says to him. "Your punishment is complete."

Softly, he tells her. "Fuck me Madam."

She leans over and kisses the top of his head whispering to him. "Later, baby. You did good." She picks up his briefs hands them to him, then scoops up his clothes and flitters away.

He looks at me with a sheepish grin as he puts his underwear on. "Seary!"

I turn to the others and say. "I may be a virgin to the swinger lifestyle but I am no virgin to sexual stimulation."

Bella starts to clap, then everyone joins in. I step off the platform and strut to Darren rubbing my hands together in rhythm to my step. *Showtime!*

CHAPTER NINE

"OK, let's take a break while we gather the things I need."

TD rubs his ass as he walks up to join everyone. "God damn! That hurt like hell."

Mac says, "Cowgirl, you best repeat your rules. I can't remember a damn thing you said after all that."

I laugh. "Rule #1: No touching me; Rule #2: No touching each other until I say GO; Rule #3: No touching yourself unless I say so; Rule #4: You may only say four phrases, Go, Baby, Go; Faster, Bitch, Faster; Fuck me! Fuck yeah! Rule #5: With every orgasm, you will say, scream, or shout Seary, that's S, E, A, R, Y; Rule #6: We will play Gorilla at the end of the night. Everyone plays. No exceptions. I'll explain those rules when we play, but here's the twist. The last one to orgasm wins and he or she will shout GORILLA! The first one to orgasm loses and they forfeit their right to pick partners for the next full year! Rule #7: If you break the rules, you will be spanked. Rule #8: If you don't apply the discipline appropriately, you will also be disciplined."

Mac nods. "OK. Got it."

"Since I'm an erotic entertainer, I thought I would entertain you tonight. Is everyone good with that?"

Everyone is smiling at me.

Darren answers with "Fuck yeah!"

"That's the right answer. I like an enthusiastic crowd."

Charlie tells everyone. "I don't know about enthusiastic, but I'm horny as hell now."

"So here's my idea. This will be a group meeting, no private sessions. I will choose the pairing. I will entertain y'all, which will consist of dancing for you both as a group and some individual lap dances."

"Oh, oh, oh." Mandy raises her hand.

I laugh, remembering she is only 20. "Yes Mandy?"

"Can Charlie have a lap dance, please? He really wants one. I tried, but I'm really not good at it." She looks lovingly at him and he gives her his best playboy smile. She looks back at me. "Pretty please?"

"Sure, Charlie gets a lap dance for Mandy." She jumps up and down, tits bouncing, then flings her arms around his neck and lays a big loud smooch on him making everyone laugh.

"The last thing we will do is play Gorilla. It will be the grand finale. Has anyone played before?"

Everyone shakes their heads. "Never heard of it."

"It's an erotic game with some B thrown in."

TD frowns. "As in BDSM? Explain."

"Surely you know what BDSM stands for? Bondage, Dominance …?"

"Of course, I know what it stands for. Explain how the B will be used."

"Well, you never know." I laugh, teasing him. "In a nutshell, Gorilla is fondling, caressing, licking, kissing, sucking and sometimes fucking your partner or partners and them doing the same in return, while maybe blindfolded and maybe tied to them. I'll watch each of you tonight and come up with something customized to get you off. That's my specialty. And I'm really, really good at it."

Mac slaps Rosa's ass and she giggles. "Fuck yeah!"

Darren laughs, and bows to me. "I am speaking for the group when I say, Seary, you can do whatever you want."

"Thank you, Darren. I guarantee you will all enjoy it very much. I aim to please." I look around at each member. "So, are there any objections to being blindfolded and restrained? It can be scary the first time you are tied up."

Rosa stomps her foot. "Finally, someone gets it!"

Brad puts his arms around Bella. She smiles at me. "We need a little scare to get our juices flowing. It'll be fun."

Angela shakes her head. "No, no objections here." And everyone else agrees, but TD looks unsure.

"TD, don't look so scared."

"I'm not scared." He crosses his arms in front of his chest.

"I assure you, the best orgasm you will ever have is blindfolded with bondage after watching an experienced, sexually explicit, erotic dancer; But I tell you what, if you are still unsure when the time comes, you can sit out and watch the others scream Seary, after their incredible orgasms. You don't have to be fucked tonight."

"Oh hell, no! I'm getting fucked tonight!"

Everyone laughs. "Attaboy!" Charlie thumps him on the back.

"That's what I thought." I smirk.

Bella tells us. "It's true about good sex after watching it live. Brad and I went out to Vegas for a little extra spice and caught the Crazy Horse Paris show, Zumanity, and Fantasy. It was a real turn on watching it live. We had the best sex in years, didn't we?"

"I was saying, Go, Baby, Go! Faster, Bitch, Faster! Fuck me!" Brad points at me.

Bella points at him. "All while I was screaming Fuck Yeah! And we weren't blindfolded!"

I explain to the group. "The mind is the most powerful aphrodisiac. Let your imagination fill it with the fantasy a live dancer will stimulate. One of the easiest ways to do that is to help the imagination focus by being blindfolded. If I choose that for you, it will be exquisite, but regardless I will create for each of you your own fucking fantasy."

Darren narrows his eyes. "Fucking Fantasy? I … know that term." He looks at me curious, then he exclaims. "My God! Are you a dancer in Vegas?"

"Yes."

"At Been Jammin'?"

"Yes."

"I'll be damned!" He tells the others pumping his fist. "Y'all, this little lady is the headliner at Been Jammin'. Seary! Wow! What a coincidence!"

I smile at him, then at everyone because their mouths have fallen open.

He tells us. "Bart is a Frat Bro of mine. He called me up a couple of years ago to tell me he had discovered a dancer who could dance circles around his other performers and he was going to turn her raw talent into a gold mine. Her name was Seary and she was a southern girl from Alabama."

I laugh. "Bart is a Frat Brother? It's a small world, isn't it? Have you seen me dance before?"

"No, we haven't been to Vegas. But Angela's been hounding me about going to see the pole dancers."

I smile at her. "We have the best in the world there. And you would love the Cirque du Soleil shows."

Darren tells her. "We're going next week, baby. I will clear my calendar for you." She throws her arms around his neck and kisses him.

"Yep, Bart's been after me to invest in a new venture he and Seary were putting together called Fucking Fantasies. He told me he was raising capital and wanted to know if my venture capitalist friend and I would be interested in going in on the ground level."

"Have you?"

"Well, as a matter of fact, I did. My buddy, who also owns rental properties out there, went to check you out. My local bro said he fell in love with you the first time he saw you dance and you were definitely a winner. So, I invested."

"Well, I'll be damned. So, we're business partners?" I stick my hand out to shake his. "Nice to meet you."

He laughs and shakes my hand. "Likewise."

"And you're local bro, the venture capitalist? Did he invest too? Do I have another business partner from around here I don't know about?"

"No, he decided not to. He said it would pose a conflict of interest and he didn't want it to blow up in his face. He said he had other plans for you."

"His loss." I shrug. *I'll have to ask Bart what other plans are in the works.*

Bella asks me. "What kind of dancing do you do exactly?"

"I do all of it. My niche is dance interpretation for maximum stimulation, but let's not talk the night away. I'd rather show you."

TD claps his hands together. "Yes, let's get to it! Please! Fucking Fantasies sounds fantastic." Everyone laughs at his charming manners.

"Before we start the party, I will need a few things for Gorilla."

I turn to the women. "Ladies, I will need blindfolds, restraints of some sort for bondage and bring all your toys in here and put them on top of the counter so I can see what you have."

Rosa takes Angela by the arm. "Come on. Let's go. My room has everything we need."

Mandy says, "I'll get the toys out."

"Darren, I have a special playlist. Can you input it into your music system?"

"Yes, I can. What is it?"

"It's my special compilation, Siri's Heart." We walk over to the TV. "Can I operate it by Bluetooth?"

"You sure can. Tap this ear piece like this." He demonstrates how to loop a song, or skip, or pause the songs, simply by tapping it. It's state of the art.

I insert the earpiece in my ear. It is lightweight and tight. *I don't think I will sling it off working the pole.* "What about the spotlights? Can you set them to track only me?"

"Sure can. Go stand under it, and I'll have it identify you, then when the music starts it will find you and stay on you. You can also operate the lights by the Bluetooth." He instructs me on how to remotely operate them too.

"Perfect."

I walk to the middle of room under the spotlight while Darren sets it up. The other men are standing close by, shooting the shit, waiting for the show to start. "Gentlemen, if you would be so kind, I need your muscles, please." They walk over. "Charlie, find me a short legged chair or stool that I can give you a lap dance on, then put it over there." I point to the area in front of the pole platform.

"Yes ma'am!"

"Mac, you too. I think you might get a special dance tonight also. Get a chair you are comfortable sitting in and put it next to the platform. It needs to be sturdy with arms, but not a big heavy piece of furniture."

"Yes ma'am!"

Brad and TD are left looking at me, awaiting instructions, but when I don't give them any, TD walks to the cabinet gets a smoke and goes out to the balcony. Brad and I watch him for a few moments in silence, then I point at the cameras in the corners of the ceiling. "Do those work?"

"Yes."

"You should record what happens here tonight." He gives me a direct, searching look not sure what I mean. "Let me rephrase that. You will *want* to record what happens here tonight, because you will want to watch my show over and over again."

He relaxes smiling a very sexy smile. "Confidence is sexy, Seary."

"It isn't just confidence, Brad. It's a proven track record perfected in front of live audiences in Vegas. I am going to rock your world!"

He chuckles. "Cockiness is sexy too!"

Scanning the room, I see that Charlie and Mac have returned with suitable chairs, but the women have not. TD is coming back inside with a drink in his hand. He walks around the room basking in the fact that he is the only one half naked. He runs his fingers through his hair, leaning his head back then shaking it loose, flexing his abs. He reaches down and checks his package. His conversation with Rachael comes back to me, and I'm concerned at his flippant attitude towards the whole situation, so I tell Brad. "You know what? Start recording now."

"Ok. Let me tell Darren. He will record everything that happens within the compound. We have cameras everywhere."

"Thanks."

"Sure, Seary. No problem." He walks to Darren and I watch them talking. Brad points to the cameras and Darren nods.

I stand alone for a minute or so and run through what dances I will give them. *It's a good time to get back in the groove, dust the cobwebs off, and grease the rusty spots. I'll open with my speech, then start the dancing with Circus by Britney, then move to ... I* rehearse my lineup. I hear Darren speak in my earpiece. "We are live and recording, Seary. Can you hear me?"

I smile, giving him the thumbs up. When I look back, TD is standing next to me posing and preening. "Seary, do you hire out by the hour, or by the night?"

"I beg your pardon?" I'm pissed immediately, knowing what he is thinking. *Whore.* I sigh. No matter how many times it happens to me, no matter how many times I get called that horrible name, it still hurts. I rattle off my usual speech, knowing it won't do any good. Once they label you, there is no going back, but I tell him anyway. "TD, I'm an erotic entertainer only. I don't fuck for money. I'm all about sex, but what I actual do isn't sex. What I actually do is dance. What I do is fantasy. What I do is only suggestive seduction. I'm not a porn star. I'm an erotic dancer. There's a big difference. Erotic is about sexual desire, and sexual excitement. I'm not a whore."

He stares at his drink then twirls the liquid. The ice cubes clink against the glass.

"If erotic dancing makes me a whore in your eyes, what does being a swinger make the wives? Are they all whores too? Words mean things, TD. Don't be a sheep. Be an independent thinker. Make up your own mind. Don't assume the labels other people place on those they wish to hold down and oppress; be your own man. Think for yourself. Be courageous and choose your own path. Each of the people here tonight have done exactly that. After tonight, you be your own judge of my profession."

TD doesn't say anything but extends his hand opening it to show me my hair clip. I look at it for a few moments, then take it. "Thanks. And for the record, whore is not a bad word and whores are not bad people. They are as good as anyone. They are real people, with real feelings. I prefer the term prostitute. Words mean things." He looks away for a moment, sees Charlie standing alone, and walks off to speak to him. I shake my head. *The magnitude of the ignorance. I can't wait to get back to Vegas!* Twisting my hair, I return it to the clip.

Brad walks back up. His smile freezes when he sees my eyes hurt, cold and hard.

"Seary, are you alright? You look …." He watches my face intently.

"I'm fine. There's a little chill in the air. Is everything running as we discussed?"

"Yes, it is." He answers still frowning at me.

"Good." I smile at him sweetly.

We stand there in silence. "As soon as you move, the tracking will activate."

"Perfect!"

When the women return to the playroom, they are all laughing. Bella has her arm around Mandy, who is tucking a titty back into her dress. Rosa tells everyone. "Mandy tried my nipple clamp then couldn't get it off. Bella had to come to her rescue."

Rosa and Angela have their arms filled with various fabrics and actual handcuffs. They take them to the counter and lay them down while Mandy and Bella bring a few toys.

Bella laughs while she tells us what happened. "I told Mandy her tits were too sensitive for them, but she insisted she try them. She freaked out, tossing the other one and we've been searching for it the whole time."

Mandy blushes. "I thought I might like them, but that was way too intense!" She rubs her nipple. "Rosa, how can you stand them?"

Rosa laughs. "It's the pain that's the turn on."

Darren starts the YouTube music videos as soon as they walked in. The first one is Rihanna's, "Pour It Up." Everyone gathers in front of the TV watching the sexy pole dancing in it. I make my way to the counter where the restraints and toys are laying. I shift through them. There are eight actual handcuffs, some lined with leopard fur, then there are some modified bungee cords, some soft rope, a lot of silk neckties, a lot of silk pillow cases, a couple of studded dog collars, a couple of leashes, regular nipple clamps, the usual dildos, a few vibrators, and Ben Wa balls. *I can see why Brad was starting to get bored.* I remember Bella said some toys were in the cabinets, so I plunder around and in the bottom right cabinet by the door, I discover some new, unopened toys. *Oh yeah! Now we are talking.* Inside are a handful of silicone cock rings, several ram cock kits, several sets of anal beads, butt plugs, Shock Therapy nipple clamps, and a bondage bar. But the real prizes, the treasures, are shoved in the back, opened, but unused. I find a couple of Lovense Max and Noras, along with 2 iPhones. A couple of Real Touch male masturbators with a pc laptop and The Joy Stick dildos. *Awesome! And not one but two rideable Sybian's, complete with the dildo attachment too! FANTASTIC! You guys are in for the time of your life tonight. I'm so excited!*

The second video is Beyoncé's "Partition."

I turn to look at Angela. *I need to have a heart to heart before I start.* I walk over and touch her arm. "Can I speak to you in private please?"

"Sure, Seary." I follow her out onto the balcony. We stand next to the railing looking down onto the courtyard and out over the infinity pool to the flower garden. It looks like a giant maze from here.

"Is anything wrong?"

"Well, I need a little sexual background on everyone before I start. I want to tailor my performance to give everyone a customized experience. To ensure everyone has a mind shattering orgasm."

Angela smiles, but it doesn't go to her eyes. *Should I start there? No. I'll come back to her.*

"For instance, I'm already familiar with Charlie and Mandy. I know Charlie likes to watch Mandy having sex with other men."

"Yes."

"Does Mandy fuck so he can watch or does she fuck and he watches."

"I see what you're asking. She fucks and he watches."

"Does she fuck him afterwards?'

"No. His chosen partner fucks him either before or after. Everyone has an orgasm. Those are the rules."

"Ok. Brad and Bella. Bella is easy to please. She orgasms at will but Brad is getting bored."

"Yes. I would say that is true. Darren and I have wondered how much longer they will stay in the group."

"Rosa and Mac. They both like it rough."

"Yes. Rosa always likes it rough. She beats herself when she is here with our men because they don't like it, but she beats Mac because I've seen his bruises."

"Ok. Does Mac get rough with the women or himself?"

"No. He is really a gentle lover. He is patient, kind, considerate. He really tries hard to please us and wants to hear us orgasm. But he does like it rough too. I've talked to him about it. He gets off on the dominate, submissive roles."

"Ok. That brings us to you and Darren. Darren seems like he would be an excellent lover."

"Yes. He is. He rescued me, you know, from a mentally abusive home." She looks away. "I don't know how I got so lucky."

"He mentioned only that you were his Fair Lady. So, you have emotional scars?"

"Had. I've been in therapy and I've been able to overcome it for the most part. Darren gives me unconditional love. He is my everything."

I smile at her. "Love heals all wounds. It truly does. So, what about being able to orgasm?"

"What about it?"

"Do you?" She looks out over the gardens and doesn't say anything. "Be truthful, Angela. Unless you have been physically damaged, you can climax and achieve an orgasm."

"No. I haven't."

"Never? How about when you were little or during your teen years with masturbation?"

"Never. I didn't do that." She looks back at me with a sincere look that touches my heart. She whispers. "I've tried! I really have!" She tears up. "I can't seem to finish so I pretend. Please don't tell the others, especially Darren. He would be heartbroken to know."

"I won't. Your secret is safe with me." I stick my hand out to shake hers. She smiles and moves to take it. I pull it back and spit in it. She laughs and does the same, and we shake. We both turn to look out over the gardens thinking. *I have to find a way to help her. She has given up on one of the greatest gifts we have. Maybe it's the pressure of knowing they expect it. Rule #8 And all. 'All parties achieve orgasm.' But maybe her needs are different from the expected norm. I have an idea!*

"Does the sound system have noise canceling headphones?"

"Yes. They are in the top cabinet over the toys."

"Great. Let's get this party started. Come on. Let's go!"

We walk back in together and Angela joins them at the TV. They are watching Madonna's "Justify My Love." Picking up the crop again, watching the end of the video as Madonna's runs away laughing, I decide how I will make my escape. *That's how I will*

222

depart tonight, but first things first. First, I have to make them love me.

I tap my earpiece as I step in front of the TV pausing the video. The screen freezes on the quote about pleasure not depending on the permission of anyone else. I address my minions. "Tonight is all about sex! Tonight is all about orgasm. Embrace it. Do *not* hold back. Release yourself from the old programing that would deny your sexual satisfaction. Let it go! Open your minds to the sensual sensations and the sexual stimulation you will feel. You have been given a most precious gift. Orgasm! Let us not shy away from it. Let us experience it. Let us embrace it. Let us celebrate it."

There is stunned silence.

I point to the left side of the room with the crop. "Men, line up." I point to the right side. "Ladies, line up." I point to TD. "TD, you are with me." He walks over and stands next to me, watching Mandy bounce to her place. I touch his arm and he leans over so I can whisper in his ear. "I want you to have each person strip down to their underwear. Start with Darren. You can use hand gestures, but you may not touch them. Put their clothes away in the cabinets. Do you understand?"

He nods and smiles. "Fuck me Madam."

I grin at him. "Are you charming me?"

"Fuck yeah."

I laugh. "TD, if you play along with everything that happens, I guarantee you are going to have the time of your life tonight. OK?"

He almost says OK, but stops himself, and grins. "Go, Baby, Go."

Turning to the group, I shout. "Are we ready?"

I hear my answers echo around the room. "Go, Baby, Go. Faster, Bitch, Faster. Fuck me. Fuck yeah!" I look at TD. "Go." Looking at the eager faces of my soon to be fans, I say. "Then let's get started."

I touch the Bluetooth. "Spotlight only." The spotlight finds me while all the other lights go off. "Play 'Circus' by Britney Spears." As the music starts I clap my hands above my head to the beat, point to myself and walk to the middle of the room. As she sings about the two kinds of people. I point to myself as the entertainer, and them as the observers. As the song continues I take on the moves of the video dancing as Britney does. When the video breaks to another dancer, I do that move too, staying as true to the original choreography as possible. *All eyes on me; I am in control; I am your ringleader!* The song lyrics reinforces my speech about letting go, and it tells them to watch, follow and show me what they can do. It's the perfect song to set the tone for the night.

Meanwhile, TD has managed in the context of charades to get Darren to understand he is supposed to strip, which he does getting naked immediately. TD points to his own underwear and Darren reluctantly puts his back on. Then TD steps to Mac and gestures to Darren and points to his clothes. He strips too. By the time he gets to Brad, everyone has figured it out and everyone's clothes come off. Even the girls strip down to their panties. No one leaves their bras on. *I like an enthusiastic crowd!*

"Blurred Lines" sung by Robin Thicke starts to play. Clapping above my head to the beat, I get everyone in the rhythm then finger wave to them to "get up" and participate. Everyone starts to clap and dance in place while TD dances back and forth carrying their clothes to the cabinets.

I strut like the models on the video in perfect step, tits bouncing through the heart of my dress to the pole. When I reach it, I casually bump and grind around it while the lyrics say there are blurred lines, good girls want to get nasty and how I know they want it. Grabbing the pole, I mount it, swing around, step down then seriously deep bump and grind it. I mount it again and shimmy to the top. Unsnapping the collar on my bodice, I push my full body off the pole and with my feet together, I swim like a mermaid in midair. The weight of the skirt pulls the dress, and it slowly slides off falling to the floor. I hang naked as my phrases are shouted and repeated from my now very enthusiastic crowd, then I grip the pole between my legs and repeat my move from earlier, diving off, pivoting, catching myself, and swinging away, but this time when I grab the pole at the bottom, I release my legs, allowing the momentum to create an open, fully extended, revolving split.

There is another group gasp, then more of my phrases. *There are def no soft dicks or dry pussies now!*

As the song starts over on a loop, I drop my legs, and let them "walk" to the floor. Standing up, I take off, bouncing my tits down the center of the floor, then take a right angle to Darren. I body flirt with him, almost touching him, but not. I squat down in front of him, jiggling my tits almost touching him, but not. He gives me a "Go, Baby, Go!"

I jump to my feet. High stepping, bouncing to Mac. I body flirt with him, almost touching, but not. I step in front of him, turn sideways, squat, fall back on one hand and hunch the air, while holding my hair up off my neck. "Faster, Bitch, Faster!"

I jump to my feet. High stepping, bouncing to Charlie. I body flirt with him, almost touching, but not. I step in front of him, I fall to my knees, arch my back, leaning all the way over as I shake my tits at him like belly dancers do. Then, I roll up, flip my hair over the top, letting it cascade around me, blow my cheeks out and puff air toward his penis. He squeals, "Fuck yeah!"

I jump to my feet. High stepping, bouncing, to Brad. I body flirt with him, almost touching, but not. I step in front of him, turn my back to him, stand shoulder width apart, drop my head to the ground, dragging my hair on the floor, then squat and twerk, and twerk, and twerk until he screams, "Fuck me! Fuck me! Fuck me!"

Now we're cooking! Bouncing my tits back to the pole, I lean on it facing them, hanging my head back I slide down the pole doing a straddle split as the song ends and the spotlight goes off.

Fuck me's and fuck yeah's ring loud around the dark room.

When the lights comes on, I am dressed again and standing in the center of the room. I motion to TD to join me by curling my finger at him, holding my other hand out for the crop. He places it in my hand. "Charlie gets his lap dance now. Put his chair in front on the floor."

TD walks up to Charlie, points at him and motions for him to follow. Charlie's dick pushes his boxers straight out and he dances behind TD singing.

"Fuck me!" I can't help but laugh. TD puts the chair at the front of the stage and Charlie settles in.

"Mandy, please come here." She bounces and flitters to me enjoying her near nakedness. I hand her the crop and wink. "Go stand behind Charlie." Grinning, she takes the crop owning it, puts it over her head and flitters to the stage. "Charlie, do you remember Rule #1?"

He frowns. "Fuck yeah." Mandy giggles.

"Good. And do you remember Rule #7?"

He pooches his lips. "Fuck yeah."

"And do you remember how good your wife is with the application of #7?"

He pouts. "Fuck yeah."

"Good. Because I remember how much she liked it too."

Mandy giggles.

"Mandy, if he raises one finger off the chair, you are to use the crop. You decide how hard and how many."

She grins and licks her lips.

Charlie says, sounding so pitiful. "Fuck me." Making everyone laugh.

I turn the lights off. In the darkness, I can hear nothing but the room breathing. Everyone is waiting to see what I do next. I tell the earpiece to play Jeff Gutt's version of "Feeling Good."

With the first strains of the music, I am bathed in the bright light, and I step with each beat crossing my legs one in front of the other like a lioness stalking her prey. I interpret the music in true stripper fashion using my hair for dramatic effect, tossing it back, then wildly swinging it to the right, then to the left. The first time Jeff starts the chorus about a new dawn, a new day and a new life, I roll up on my toes like Michael Jackson and hold it. When he sings "Feeling Good," I slide my hand between my legs and thrust my hips to the horns three times. On the fourth thrust, I pull my hand up, grabbing my skirt and exposing myself.

A slow "Go ... Baby ... Go" slips out of Charlie's mouth.

On the next verse, I square up to the chair in a strong stance, standing directly in front of him. Placing one foot between his legs, pushing against his knee with mine, forcing him to spread his legs wide, I spin around and step in, while I throw my head back letting my hair hang over his lap. I lift my arms over my head and start down slithering, spreading his legs further as my body touches them with my ass rolling in my dress like a heartbeat. When I reach the bottom and Jeff sings, "Feeling Good" again, I spin around and blow a concentrated stream of air onto his straining dick pushing against the thin fabric as the horns play.

He grips the arms on the chair, leans his head back and screams. "Fuck me!" I know he wants to touch me or himself. His eyes come back immediately to me and I grin wickedly at him, licking my lips. His knuckles are white with the strain of maintaining control.

On the third verse, I start the same slow sexy slither back up as Jeff sings about dragonflies and butterflies, running my hands over my body, and into my hair. Unsnapping my collar, I leave my hands holding it until he sings that there is a new, bold world for me. That's when I lean over Charlie's lap letting my top drop off my tits and I swing them forward at his face. His hands start to twitch. As Jeff draws out "meee...eeee....eeee...," I squeeze them while rolling my head around my shoulders.

Charlie roars. "FUCK YEAH! FUCK ME!"

The music shifts again, and I lower my head till my hair lays on his lap, then I throw my hair, whipping it around and around in a frenzy. As the words express not having freedom and understanding that feeling, I use my hair to tickle his skin, flipping it and dragging it over his face, down his chest then over his cock held captive.

Charlie moans.

Mandy says, "Go, Baby, Go."

At the end of the song, Gutt sings about a new dawn, a new day and a new life. The first time, I throw my hair back, thrust my tits at him and wink. Then I stand up, turn around, cock my ass and push my skirt off one side of my hip. Cocking my hip to the other side, I push my skirt off that side. It slides off and lays in a pile at Charlie's feet. As I prance to the middle of the room, I pose to each dramatic beat. On the last "feeling good" chorus, I dig my fingers in one butt cheek and one breast squeezing hard, while I spin around as the song ends in darkness.

I turn the spotlights on the pole platform. Charlie and Mandy have not moved. Charlie is breathing hard and still has a death grip on the chair when I walk back up to retrieve my dress.

I slip it back on as he sits and continues to watch my every move. Pulling the dress up, wiggling my hips as the skirt slides up. I bend over and pull the bodice over my tits and snap the hook. When I'm dressed, I fluff my hair and place my stiletto on his knee then lean over to him. "Tell me Charlie, did you like your lap dance?"

He throws his head back and crows like a rooster. "Fuck yeah!"

When Mandy does the same thing, everyone laughs, and I drop my heel, spin around. "That's what I thought." *I'm owning it!*

Mandy comes around to the front of the chair with the crop and waves it at him and to the men's line. She tells him. "Go, Baby, Go."

He pushes up out of the chair, his erection stands straight out at full attention. He can't resist the urge to say. "I'm feeling fucking good!" Mandy rears back and swats his ass with the crop making him jump and yipe. "Fuck …." And quickly adds. "Yeah!"

She giggles as she hands the crop back to me and they return to their side of the lines. She bouncing and flittering as only she can do and he strutting his erection as only he would do.

Before I return to the center of the room, I motion again for TD to come to me. When he arrives, I hand him the crop. "Wait here for me." He jumps onto the platform and I walk under the center spotlight.

When I'm there, I turn the spotlight off. Darkness and silence fall over the room again. Only the sound of their excited breathing fills the air. I take my time, letting the anticipation build, closing my eyes and becoming Britney Spears. I haven't done this routine in a while, but I know when I hear the music, the dancer will remember every move as if it were yesterday.

The first strands of "I'm A Slave For You" starts, the spotlight comes back on and for the next 3:23 minutes, they watch Britney dance the video. Every body thrust, every hip grind, every fucking move is perfect. *The dance is upon me! I don't deny it. I don't hide it.* When it's over, there is spontaneous applause. "I thank you and Britney thanks you."

Pointing at TD, he comes trotting to me. Whispering in his ear, I tell him what is up next. He turns to Mac and motions for him to follow. They pick up the lap dance chair he selected and move it behind the stripper pole facing the room. Mac takes a seat, places his hands on his knees, not on the arms of the chair, as instructed, gives a mighty "Fuck yeah!" which sounds like yee-haw and waits, grinning.

Rosa jumps up and down knowing she is going to get to participate. I motion for her to join him. She takes the crop and stands behind Mac like Mandy did. "Quick learners."

The others chuckle and Charlie says, "Faster, Bitch, Faster."

As I hit the Bluetooth to turn off the center spotlight and turn on only the lights on the stage, I step out of my stilettos. When Chris Cagle's, "Let

There Be Cowgirls" starts, I sprint to the stage. Using Charlie's lap dance chair as a catapult, I propel myself at the pole. Grabbing it, I swing my legs straight out, letting my momentum carry them over the top of Mac's head. He blinks and twitches out of instinct but he doesn't move. He holds his ground, fearless.

Rosa lets out a Cowgirl "Fuck yeah!" As she ducks and takes a step back.

The revolution brings me to his chair, and I lightly place my feet on each arm, towering over him. I dance like I'm riding a horse, swaying, dipping, hunching and grinding. When I look down on him, Mac grins that sexy sideways grin and I see Matthew McConaughey. Matthew and I have some early history in my career so I decide to give Mac a fucking fantasy ride. I grin wickedly back at him and he leans his head back. "Fuck yeah!" *Def a Matthew move.*

When Chris says "Ow, come on," I unsnap my dress and let it slide down again. I kick it off and grin down at him. His python hardens and peeks out of the top of his briefs. I crank up my dance. Then, right before the chorus, I bend over, legs straight, ass in the air, tits dangling in front of him, I take his hands, place them over his python. "So." He grins understanding Rule #3 as he strokes it.

234

When "Let There Be Cowgirls" is sung, I drop down onto the arms of the chair, straddling it. "Fuck me!" Mac shouts as I ride, grinding just over his hands. He strokes his cock to the rhythm of my gait and moans softly with a sexy drawl only to me. "Faster, Bitch, Faster."

Rosa, however, shouts. "Go, Baby, Go!"

When Cagle sings about the first time he sees the girl, knowing Mac's breathing is going to be panting before too much longer, I tell him. "Whoa, now." He stops his ride as I slide my ass to the left, swing my right leg off, up over his head and unseat the saddle. Returning to the pole, with my back to it and him, I grab it over my head and pull, lifting my legs up and over my head. At the top, I separate them into a split and drop them one at a time onto the arms of the chair. Lunging immediately for the pole, I climb to the top and pole dance like it's a trick pony. Then I push away, open my legs in a straddle split over his head giving both, he and Rosa, an eye full of my delightful diva-ness as I slowly slide down the pole to the chair.

Mac lets out a shrill whistle.

Rosa whispers in awe of my in air flexibility. "Fuck me."

When the lyrics say how badly he hurt as a teenager watching her ride, I drop onto the arms of the chair again sitting with my thighs spread wide and ride his imaginary horse hard. Grabbing his shoulders, I hunch directly over his crotch, riding that chair fast and hard like the Cowgirl I am. I see the strain starting from resisting me. I push him to his limits by throwing my left hand up and in true Rodeo fashion, I mimic bull riders lifting myself up and letting myself down, over and over again. My tits bouncing and flouncing wildly. For more than 8 seconds, I manage to stay on his bull before he bellows. "FASTER, BITCH, FASTER!" I drop my left hand down as I thrust my tits into his face, but right before they touch him, my hand shoots out, grabbing his throat, squeezing it, choking him. I rope him forcing his head back as I pull my body up his, so close I stir his chest hairs. I pin him until I am able to stand back up on the arms of the chair. His face straining, getting redder and redder.

Rosa let's out a scream. "FUCK YEAH!" As she proceeds to whip her own ass with the crop. "GO, MOTHERFUCKER, GO!"

When I release Mac, he gasps for air then let's out a bellowing. "GO, BABY, GO! DON'T STOP NOW! GOD DAMN! I GOTTA FUCK SOMETHING!" When he reaches for me, I twist, jump and grab the pole, swinging away before he violates my Rule #1. Rosa steps forward and lays the crop down on his chest with a smashing blow. He screams. "FUCK ME!"

She screams. "FUCK YEAH!" Over and over again, she punishes him.

I shimmy up the pole, riding the top again for the Rodeo as the last drums beat, and when the whistle is heard, I wrap my leg and fall mimicking a roped calf. I dangle as the song ends, watching as Rosa stops shocked and Mac slumps in the chair.

Fuck! I hope he is all right! She whipped him hard! There are welts. She has got to rein that frustrated passion in.

No one says anything. You can hear a pin drop. There is only the sound of Rosa's shallow rapid panting and Mac's deep gasping. When I dismount the pole, I squat next to him put my hand on his arm and ask softly if he is ok. With his eyes closed, he says, "Seary!"

I tell Rosa as I pat his arm. "Let's give him a minute." He grins without opening his mouth for me in a silent thank you and I hear her smacking her lips. *What is she doing?* Standing, I turn to her and she grins at me with a wild but happy look in her eyes. He has shot her with a direct hit and she is cleaning herself by licking her fingers as she wipes his semen off her body. *Damn! That's true love!*

As I gather my dress, slip it back on and watch them silently, she squats by Mac's side. With a tone and inflection that says I'm sorry, she says to him. "Fuck yeah! Fuck me!" Then she stands and kisses him on the top of his head, waiting patiently for him to recuperate.

He inhales deeply and pulls himself out of the chair. He grabs her hand and raises their arms in victory. "FUCK YEAH!" Then he turns them to me and they bow.

I turn on all the lights for them as they make their way back to the line. The others start clapping. Mac's python is tamed and Rosa walks quiet and subdued. When she gets to Angela, she gets a much needed hug.

"TD, bring my shoes, please." He does as instructed and as I slip them. "It's your turn." I hook his arm and take him to the ladies. "Ladies, where are my manners? I haven't properly introduce TD to you yet. Here are your rules." I show him off like a piece of meat. "You can touch TD anywhere and everywhere, except his cock, on my count of 30. I might count fast or I might count slow, so you ladies make this examination count."

When Carlito Olivero's version of Satisfaction starts to play, I position TD directly in front of

Angela. I stand behind him so he can't see me. "Ok, Angela. Ready, get set, go!"

TD smiles at her. "Go, Baby, Go."

I encourage her. "Don't be bashful, Angela. Touch him."

He lifts his eyebrows, grins and teases her.

She drops down to her knees in front of him. She puts both hands on the outside of his legs.

"Oh, dear. I forgot to start counting. One…."

She runs her hands inside his briefs over his ass and cups his butt, then squeezes it.

"Two…."

She pulls her hands to the front and then slides them on the sensitive inside of his thigh forcing his legs apart. I speed up the counting. By the time I reach 9, she has pushed her hand between his legs and is rubbing his balls. His cock gets hard and he grins at her. She grins at him too, while she strokes them. When I reach 20, one hand is tickling his balls while the other is massaging his ass and he is pulsating his cock for her in time to the music. The last 10 seconds, she slides her hand between the crack of his ass and down to meet her other hand. She cups his balls with both hands as she blows a tight stream of hot air on his cock. *That is a good technique, right there. Well played.*

He leans his head back with a look of sheer ecstasy on his face.

"30. Time is up."

When she stands, he steps up to her. "Fuck me?"

She smiles. "Fuck yeah!"

I move him with the crop to Rosa. "Same instructions, Rosa. Go." Rosa spins him around and steps up behind him, putting his ass into her crotch. She slides her hands down his back to his ass and squeezes his cheeks, pinching them. She grins at Angela and nods. "Fuck yeah." Then she slides her hands around his abs and belly slaps him. He tightens them, and she taps them, testing the hardness. I count a steady beat as she proceeds to move around the front checking him as if he were a stallion she is buying for breeding. She checks his ears, his teeth, his hands and even his feet. At 25, she stands in front and bends over, exposing her pussy to him and taps her own ass indicating she wants to be mounted and bred.

He tells her. "Fuck yeah! Faster, Bitch, Faster. Fuck me! Go, Baby, Go."

On 30, she pats him on the side of the cheek. "Fuck me?"

He answers grinning. "Fuck yeah!"

They grin at each other until I push him away to Mandy. When TD's eyes land on her, he forgets

Angela and Rosa. His eyes light up and he gives her his version of the sexy sideways smile and winks at her. "Fuck me!"

"We all know what TD wants of Mandy, but what will Mandy want of TD?"

Someone on the men's side can't hold back his snickering and it burst out of his lips, then there is laughter from the men. Mandy rolls her eyes at the guys, but starts to giggle then she bats her eyes at TD. Even, the other ladies start to giggle and laugh. *This should be good.*

When I give her permission to start, TD gives her a little eyebrow pump. "Faster, Bitch, Faster, Fuck me!" Mandy reaches for his hair and pulls his face to hers. He closes his eyes and opens his mouth fully expecting to be kissed on the lips, but instead, she turns his head and proceeds to give him the sexiest wet willie ever!

I can't believe what I'm seeing! I turn to face the men, put my hands in the air. "Does Mandy have a fetish?"

"FUCK YEAH's" echo from them, followed by laughter again. I turn back to watch her tongue fuck his ear, laughing with the rest of them. I am so shocked, I forget to count. She has his head in a head lock, secured by his hair. She traces her tongue all around his ear; she flicks her tongue on the earlobe;

she thrusts her tongue in and out of his ear hole. All to the beat of the song. "This is the perfect song!" I start to bounce and clap to the music, encouraging everyone to join in. We all dance, palm pumping the ceiling till the end of the song. They stop but I don't. I know it's on loop. When the song starts over again, the guys roar with laughter because Mandy hasn't stopped her ear fucking and the sound of sucking and slobbering is getting loud. She is thoroughly enjoying it.

TD lets out a strained, "Fuck ... me!"

Damn! "Ok! Ok! Stop, stop! I can't breathe. Mandy that's enough ear love. 30, dear, 30." Mandy wipes her mouth with the back of her hand. She has the most deliciously, wicked look on her face with her flushed cheeks.

TD looks around for something to dry his ear; anything to wipe it with. I wag my finger at him. "Ah, NO!" Everyone is still laughing as he gives up the hunt, letting the slobber run down his neck, laughing with the rest of us.

She apologizes to him with her big round eyes and a sweet face. "Fuck me?"

He laughs and gives her an 'I'm a good sport' look. "Fuck yeah!"

When we step over to Bella, I tease him. "I wonder what surprises Bella has for you." She smiles at TD, pushes a stray strand of hair from her face and sets her attitude to match her smile. When the song starts to play, she cuts her eyes and raises her eyebrows at me. It's Katy Perry's, "I Kissed A Girl." I shrug innocently and turn to the others. "I didn't do that, but hey, let's roll with it."

I push TD to the side with the crop. "Stand right there." I take Bella's hand and lead her to where TD was standing in front of Mandy for the wet willie. "Bella kiss Mandy." She takes one look at Mandy's frightened face and hesitates. "No? Ok." I turn around and ask the men what they think. "What say you guys, should Bella kiss Mandy?"

Brad hasn't finished saying "Fuck yeah" before Charlie chimes in and Mac starts a chant of "Go, Baby, Go." Which they all do until I lift my hands for silence.

I turn to Bella. "Looks like this is going to happen. Can you do it?" She nods as her eyes twinkle at me. But Mandy's blue eyes are big as saucers. She is unsure about this idea. I step up to her and stand toe to toe, breast to breast with her. "Mandy, do you trust me?" She nods. "Ok then, lean your head back, put your palms over your eyes, and relax. Now, no peeking until I say so." I motion to the others for complete silence. She leans her head back, puts her palms to her eyes and takes a deep breath. I lean in close and whisper in her ear. "TD's going to get you warmed up first, is that ok?" She smiles and nods. I take the crop and rub her nipples with it. She takes a sharp intake of air.

I look at Bella and point to Mandy's tits. She grins but tries to hide it. She might be able to resist kissing Mandy's lips, but she can't resist her tits. TD shifts his position so he can see better. She steps forward, opens her mouth into a pucker, places her lips on Mandy's nipple and tickles her with light lip pressure. Mandy sucks in air sharply, causing her chest to expand. Bella proceeds to show the whole room how hot lesbian love is. Her mouth and tongue work their magic on both tits swapping and taking turns until the tips of her nipples are hard and long from the puckering, licking, flicking, sucking, rolling, and teasing. Bella goes nonstop while Mandy's start to pant. Then biting her lip, she spurts the words. "No…." She twists her head. "Don't…." She squirms. "Stop!"

She tries to turn away from the exquisite tit torture but I tell her firmly. "Stay put."

She locks her legs, but tries to pull her massive tits back out of reach, while she repeats the individual commands. "No! … Don't! … Stop!" But Bella increases the passionate play, rolling her tongue around and around them, then dragging the nipple with a flat tongue on one long lick, making Mandy groan. "No! Please!" She throws her head back and forth between each word. "Don't!" She opens and closes her fingers on her face. "Stop!" Mandy starts to quiver and Bella bites down gently, dragging her teeth from the base to the tip and at the end pinching it. Mandy squeals and thrusts her breasts forward. Bella moves to the other breast and repeats biting down gently, dragging her teeth from the base to the tip and pinching the end of the other nipple. Mandy puts her head back and arches her back. "Fuck yeah!" Bella nibbles the nipples biting them then flicking her tongue rapidly over the ends making Mandy's pussy twitch. Mandy gives a gurgling moan, growling. The room is quiet but for the sound of heavy panting when Bella stops abruptly and waits. Mandy screams out. "NOOOOO! PLEASE DON'T STOP!" As she stands on her tip toes pushing up, straining for Bella's touch. Bella licks with a wide wet tongue one nipple then the other. Mandy's body is flexed and straining. Bella waits then repeats the wet lick. Mandy shivers. Bella waits then this time when she leans to lick, Mandy thrusts her tits to her begging. "Please don't stop!" Bella puckers up, puts her lips on the hard protruding nipple only and sucks hard, then she flicks it fast, while she pinches and teases the other with her fingers. Mandy's hips start to twitch again and Bella doesn't stop. She drives Mandy wild! Mandy's whole body starts to move like a wave as her tits thrust Bella and her hips thrust air. "Oh!" She strains and screams. "FUCK … I'M GOING…."

Bella stops.

"NO! NO! NO!" Mandy shakes her head. Bella steps up one last time and bites a nipple. Mandy's hips convulse and when she drops her hands from her eyes to massage her pussy, she screams. "FUCK YEAH! I'M GOING TO…." But she stops cold as she looks into Bella's shinning eyes and at her wet lips. Mandy's voice fades as she finishes her sentence. "Cum."

Now Bella steps up to the plate, and hits a home run out of the park. She reaches for Mandy, cupping her hands softly around her surprised face, and closes the short distance between them. She stares into Mandy's eyes as she turns her face up to receive her kiss. Mandy's eyes close in surrender and her mouth opens as Bella plants a full tongue kiss on her that makes the temperature in the room rise to hot as hell.

"Fuck yeah's" are heard softly from the men's line as Mandy completely surrenders to Bella's kiss. Grabbing her own tits, she pinches the nipples herself while Bella tongues her mouth. Then she slips one hand down to her pussy and rubs her own clit. When

Bella releases her mouth, Mandy looks into Bella's eyes pleading. Bella hooks her mouth back on Mandy's tit and Mandy leans her head back moaning and masturbating. Bella drives her into another frenzy and she screams, closing her eyes, losing herself completely in the moment. "Fuck me … Fuck me … Fuck me … OH … Fuck me!"

The guys chant "Faster, Bitch, Faster."

With her orgasmic spasms, Mandy's hips hunch uncontrollably as she cums. Then they twitch several times after she finishes. She stands there lost for a few moments, then she opens her eyes. "Fuck me! That was fucking fantastic!"

Bella steps back to her place in line, grinning.

Mandy looks at me. "Oops. I'm sorry. I couldn't help myself."

"We're good." I tell her as I give her a wink and Bella a nod for a job well done.

Mandy cuts her eyes at Bella. "That was incredible, Bella."

Bella winks at her too then gives me a nod.

Mandy steps out of line, grinning at the men, shoots her arms in the air in victory. "Seary!"

I love my job!

TD looks at Bella. She winks at him too. He looks back at Mandy's red tits still hard. I lean over and say to him. "Now, that's how you do it."

247

He smirks.

CHAPTER TEN

"Ok, TD, it's almost time for Gorilla. I need you to sync one Real Touch with the Joystick and the PC, and one Lovense Max and Nora with the phones so both devices are live. Plus plug both Sybians in, make sure they work and look for two extension cords. Then count out 9 headsets, 9 dark pillow cases for the blindfolds. I think we'll skip the bondage for the most part."

He smiles, thankful. "Fuck yeah."

"You're welcome. Oh, and 4 Viagras, or 5." He smiles even bigger. "When I bring everyone to you, hand the men the little blue pill, then everyone wears a headset and a blindfold. Once we dance off, take the toys and put them …." I instruct him on where I want what.

"Fuck me Madam." He saunters off to handle the task.

"Bella, do you mind if I dance with Brad?" She smiles, completely satisfied with her role tonight. "Go, Baby, Go."

"Brad, will you please join me in the center? It's your turn." I motion to him as I take center stage again and the spotlight finds me while the perimeter lights go out. Christina Aguilera, "Dirrty" plays and for the next 4 minutes, I am Christina and Brad dances with me playing different parts. *I knew you were a dancer.* He even does Redman's rap portion, some of the group dance moves, and falls on the floor so I can walk over him. At the end of the song, he braces steading himself, and I jump on him gripping his rock hard abs with my legs. He catches me perfectly, flinging his arms behind him so he doesn't touch me while I hunch his rib cage. I push off and finish the song as I wipe my lip. "What?"

Brad takes my hand, pretends to kiss it, drops to his knees and bows down worshipping me, making me laugh. He gets up and returns to his place in line, grinning. *He knows he killed it and he enjoyed himself.*

I call out. "TD, please blindfold Angela." He looks up surprised, then rummages around on the counter and grabs a silk pillow case. He walks to Angela smiling and without hesitation he puts it on her. She is silent during the whole thing completely trusting me and ready for whatever I decide to do. He looks at me and I motion for him to bring her to the stage, slowly. He stands behind her, whispers something to her, wraps his arms around her waist and pushes her forward. She lays her hands on his and walks. As he guides her to me, I say, "Darren, please grab that short stool right behind you and bring it to me here." But I motion for him to come with me to the stage and for Charlie to actually get the stool and put it in the center of the room. When he walks up to me, I point to the front of the platform and whisper. "Darren, I want you to stand right here. I'm going to have Angela stand here in front of you. When the music starts, I want you to pull the blindfold off her but don't touch her. Don't touch her! Do you understand Rule #2 and Rule #7?" He nods. "When the song is over I want you to put it back on her. I don't want her to know you are here." I put my fingers to my lips and indicate I want quiet.

He nods. I motion TD to bring Angela and put her directly in front of Darren as I say, "TD, when the music starts, please remove Angela's hood."

When he puts her on the mark, I shush him away and he walks to stand with the men as I walk back to the center of the room under the spotlight. Turning to the women, I wave them back out of the light. They collectively step back a few feet. When I turn to the men, they have already done the same. The appearance is that Angela and I are alone in the room.

"This dance started it all. It launched my career. I hope you enjoy it." Beyoncé's "Dance For You" starts and the volume is loud. Darren pulls off the pillowcase. The sound of thunder fills the air. It sounds like it is raining outside.

As I dance, I lose myself in my beloved character and dance it with all the passion for the freedom this performance has given me. And I dance it for Angela, such a sweet soul but still a virgin to the explosive power of passion and the satisfaction of orgasm. I dance to let her know she shouldn't give up on the power of love making and the power of making love. She should sit back, relax and roll with it. It isn't about performing for others, it's about enjoying yourself and letting go. I walk to her mimicking the last seconds of the video to find her spellbound. Reaching out for her hand, she gives it to me and I bring it up to my lips to kiss as if she is royalty, a queen. Darren slides the pillowcase back over her head. There is, several seconds of silence, then light applause. I walk Angela back myself to the other girls while Darren steps off the stage and returns alone and TD goes back to the counter to finish preparations for the game of Gorilla. When I remove the pillowcase, Angela has tears in her eyes. I kiss her hand again. "It's whatever you want. It's about pleasing yourself."

I skip back to the middle of the room. "IT"S TIME!" I say mimicking Bruce Buffer. I shout to the girls. "Girls? Are you ready to be 'O' so satisfied?"

"Go, Baby, Go!"

I shout to the guys. "How about you men? Are you ready to get the 'D' rocked?"

"Faster, Bitch, Faster!"

"Are you horny enough?"

"Fuck me!"

"Then let's play Gorilla!"

"Fuck yeah!"

"Gorilla" by Bruno Mars plays. As soon as the drums start, I bounce in place to the jungle tempo. One by one, I call the participants to me to form a dance train. Not by couples, but randomly. Darren first, then Bella, Charlie, Angela, Mac, Mandy, Brad and Rosa. They follow my dance rhythm moving with me to the counter where TD is waiting on us. He gives each man a Viagra then throws one up in the air and catches it in his open mouth making everyone laugh. Then he takes the headsets, fits them over the ears, being extra careful with the girls hair. And last, he throws over the pillowcases. Then he places their hands on the partner in front, one on the shoulder, one on the hip. When everyone is ready, I lean heavily to my right causing the whole line to lean and I take a step. Like a snake, everyone follows and we dance slowly around the perimeter of the room while TD runs back and forth setting everything up.

On the pole, he attaches one end of a pair of leopard padded handcuffs and attaches the other end to the spreader bar. Then, he puts one of the Sybian's facing the front of it. On his next trip, he takes the other Sybian to the back corner and turns it facing the walls. Nora is tossed on a love seat and Max on a chair with a silk tie while the Real Touch male masturbator is placed on an elevated chair and the Joystick is placed on the couch below it.

When the snake dance has reached the pole platform, I stop. Still moving to the beat of Gorilla, I take each individual by the shoulders and face them front. TD joins us and stands at the end next to Rosa with his headset on and his pillowcase thrown over his shoulder. He grins at me and faces front.

I turn all the lights off, lift Darren's blindfold up. It shrouds his face allowing him only to see straight ahead. I whisper on his lips. "Shush. Silence during the game until you can't hold it anymore and you explode with ecstasy as you call my name. Let the game begin." I repeat this same procedure and words to each one. When I reach TD, I gently place the pillowcase over his head, taking my time to touch and caress him while I adjust the shroud. Then, I lay my finger on his lips and rub them. "Shush…" and I repeat the sentence. When I finish, I trace my finger down his chin, down his chest, down his abs, stopping short of his navel, then I trace around the waist band of his briefs to his ass and pull them down, then push him one step forward so he stands naked. I do the same for each one ending with Darren.

I return to the center of the room and strip. I hold my hands over my head with my legs bent and together showing them my back. I turn the spotlight on for a count of three. Then I turn it off. The room goes dark again. I turn it on again to show my side profile bent over with my tits dangling and my face pulled up, the closest leg straight, then other bent with my arms straight, pushed back. The light goes off. Then I turn to face them and when the light comes back on, I dance. I dance the most erotic of the night. I twist, twirl, spin, hair toss, moving my hands up and down in the air, up and down my body, arching, bending, fondling myself, while I build the tempo into a fucking frenzy. The last imprint on their minds eye is a whirling tornado of hair and body accented by the light and shadows. *A fucking fantasy.* Then I turn the lights off, return to them and pull the shrouds down.

Turning only the distant lights on at the counter, I take Charlie first. I move behind him, place my hands on his hips and push him in time to the song, then I move in front, put his hands in my hair as I back up the steps onto the elevated platform. He follows me and I sit him in the chair. I reach into the pillowcase, pull the headset off, speak then return it. "When the music changes, you will pull off only your blindfold, suit up, and watch your show. This is your Fucking Fantasy." I put the Real Touch male masturbator next to him.

Returning to the group, I take Darren next. Placing his hands on me, one on my shoulder and one on my waist, I dance with him to the corner. I spin him around and push him against the wall. I reach into the pillowcase, pull the headset off, speak then return it. "When the music changes, you will pull off both your blindfold and headset, take the remote control and operate it for your partner's maximum pleasure. You will watch stoic and in complete silence. Her pleasure comes before yours. You will wait until she comes for you then you may fuck her to your heart's content. Enjoy your Fucking Fantasy."

The next placement is Brad. I take both his hands, place them on my hips and spin around letting him feel my waist as we dance to the chair where he will watch Bella. Picking up Max, I spin Brad around and push him down to sit in it. Then, reaching into the pillowcase, I pull the headset back, speak then return it. "When the music changes, you will pull off both your blindfold and headset then suit up. You will watch in complete silence. Enjoy your Fucking Fantasy show."

Returning to the group, I pull TD away by his hand and arm, I lead him to the couch, push him all the way down, making him lay down. Then, reaching into the pillowcase, I pull the headset off, speak then return it. "When the music changes, you will pull your blindfold off. You will watch in complete silence. You will be submissive to your lover. You will let her do whatever she wants. Enjoy your Fucking Fantasy."

Next, I get Bella. I pull her by the arm to the love seat. I sit her down on it and hand her the Nora. She feels of it while I reach into the pillowcase, pull the headset off, speak then return it. "When the music changes, you can start, but do not pull your blindfold off. This is a private event for your enjoyment. You are to masturbate to the music. Enjoy your Fucking Fantasy."

Mandy is starting to bounce. She is ready to start. I pull her by the arm to the couch where TD lays waiting. I sit her down, cup her face with my hand, pull the headset off, speak then return it. "When the music changes, you will pull your blindfold off, pick up the toy next to you and do whatever feels good to you and your partner to your heart's content. Enjoy your Fucking Fantasy."

"Go, Baby, Go," she whispers to me making me smile.

Next I get Rosa. I lead her by the arm to the pole platform and pull her up on stage directly behind the Sybian. I reach into her pillowcase, pull the headset off, speak then return it. "When the music changes, you will not pull your blindfold off. This is a private event for your enjoyment." I put the remote control in her hand. "When the music changes you will mount and ride, baby, ride. I expect you to have no less than 3 Seary's. See how many you can have. When you are finished pleasing yourself, you may then remove both your blindfold and headset, find and satisfy your lover. He will be completely submissive to you. You are not to dominate harshly. You are to be tender and gentle. You will drive him wild and make him beg you for release without pain, without punishment. You will make him beg you from pure passionate pleasure. Make him squirm like Bella made Mandy. You may whisper endearing words only. Enjoy your Fucking Fantasy."

Returning, I take Angela next. *I want this to be special for you.* I put my arm around her shoulder, hug her tight, then hook her hand in my arm. Leading her to the corner where I put her directly behind the

Sybian. I reach into her pillowcase, pull the headset off, speak then return it. "When the music changes, do not pull the blindfold or the headset off. The fucking fantasies are individual. When the music changes, I want you to mount, relax and ride. Focus only on your own fantasies, your own desires and your own satisfaction. Take as long as you need to. There is no need to rush. You may touch yourself in any way you secretly fantasize about to pleasure yourself. If you call my name, you do not have to stop playing Gorilla. You may please yourself as often as you want. When you are finished and fully satisfied, you may then remove both your blindfold and headset and return to the group. My dear, sweet Angela, relax. Let yourself go. Be who you are. This is your personal Fucking Fantasy."

And, the last one to put in place is Mac. Placing his hands on me, one on my shoulder and one on my waist, I dance with him to the pole platform. Before I step up, I take his hands and move them to my face then into my hair. When I step up and back, he follows, stepping up and forward to the pole. There, I spin us around so his back is to it. Removing his hands from my hair, I drag them over my jaw, putting the palms together, then controlling them down, allowing the backs to brush my cleavage. Then, I raise them up to his head where I leave them in his hair. I walk around to the pole, raise the bondage bar that TD attached to it with a pair of handcuffs earlier and clamp each of Macs wrists. He can slide the bondage bar up and down the pole for comfort, but he can't get away. I reach into the pillowcase, pull the headset off completely. "When the music changes, listen in complete silence to the sounds of passion and orgasm around you. Pay special attention to your lover. She will be right here on the platform with you. When she comes to you, you will be completely submissive to her. You are not to speak; you are only to enjoy. This is your Fucking Fantasy."

I survey the room of Swingers satisfied as I put my dress back on. As the song "Gorilla" ends, I turn all the spotlights on. Each couple is bathed in bright, blinding light. *Good.* They can see only what is immediately in front of them. The shadows are distinct. *Let the game begin.* My edited version of "Freebird" by Lynard Skynard fills their headsets and fills the room. The song in my playlist begins at the 4:40 mark and loops back to the 5:00 mark for an hour. Which is longer than any Fucking Fantasy has ever lasted.

Smiling, I watch as Charlie, Mandy, and TD pull their blindfolds off. They look at each other and grin. Charlie slides his erection into the Real Touch masturbator. "Fuck yeah!" Mandy picks up the

Joystick, looks at him and licks it. He squeals. "Go, Baby, Go." She puts it in her mouth and he thrusts his hips. "Fuck me!" She cuts her eyes at TD and grins. She holds the Joystick in her mouth as she crawls on top of TD. He lays still completely submissive to her. She puts her breasts in his face. He takes one in his mouth and proceeds to enjoy them while Mandy sucks the Joystick and Charlie watches, enjoying via remote stimulation. *They are enjoying their gorilla.*

I look to Mac and Rosa. He is standing very straight and still, listening to the sound of the Sybian humming. She plays with the speeds and settles on the highest setting. The machine thumps as she sits it, riding it hard. Her moans are loud and long. As I look to Angela and Darren, I hear Rosa's first orgasm. "SEARY!" *That's one.*

When I focus on Angela and Darren, I see that she hasn't mounted yet. She is running her fingers over it. *Come on, Darren. Hit the remote. She is looking to turn the damn thing on.* He realizes it about the same time, and turns it on low. She sits on it and immediately puts her hands on the front bracing, leaning over it. When she picks her head up, the strain on her face is obvious. She is trying so hard to orgasm, but it isn't happening. She bursts into tears, sobbing. He stands stoic as instructed but I know it is hard for him. He has rescued her from so much. He waits and watches as the sobs rack her body. When she is finished crying, she tries again determined. Darren keeps the speed on low. She sits again enjoying the feeling, but not expecting any fireworks. Darren increases the speed and she leans her head back. He keeps increasing the speed until she stands up. Then he turns it down a little and she sits on it again. Her hips start to hunch, her hand goes to her nipple and she teases herself, but still no panting, still no climax building orgasm.

I turn to look over at Brad and Bella. He is watching her masturbate, but doesn't have on the Max. He is holding it in his hand. I walk quickly up to him as I hear Rosa shout my name again, laughing. I give him a look of 'what the fuck's the problem here' and he gives me a look that says I'm not putting my precious dick inside that. "Fine. I'll fuck you myself."

Walking to the counter, I pass Darren. He has a condom and a tube of lube in his hand. *What's happening in the corner with Angela?* Grabbing my purse, which I sling over my shoulder, I also grab a cock ring, a pair of handcuffs, the dog collar, and a leash which I attach to the dog collar as I walk back to Brad. When I step up behind him, I quietly secure the leash to the chair and ready the dog collar and handcuffs after I drop the cock ring over his shoulder into his lap. "Put this on, then I'm going to fuck you till you can't walk." He grins, drops Max to the floor and slides the cock ring on his now erect cock. When he lifts his head up, I slip the dog collar quickly around his neck and pull the belt tight. He reaches his hands up to it as he tries to stand. I slap a cuff on and hook him to the leash which has him pinned to the chair. When he jerks it, it tightens on his collar, choking him. He starts to laugh. "Fuck me." Stepping around to face him, he relaxes and gives me a not as confidant, but still bored look.

I smirk at him. "I changed my mind. This is your last chance. Put the device on your cock. And remember everything that happens within this house is confidential. Everything."

He shakes his head at me, defiant.

Now I laugh, nodding confident. I reach into my purse and pull my gun out. Standing between him and the others, I use my body to block their view while I show it to him. "It's real."

His eyes narrow slightly, but he recovers quick, looking less confidant, but still bored.

Ah, you don't think it's real. Emptying the bullets into my hand, I show them to him. "These are real too."

His face remains lax, but his eyes are alert.

Ah, you don't think I'll do it. I raise an eyebrow at him and stare him down. He meets my stare and I laugh again. "You don't know me, Brad. I'm wild at heart." I drop the bullets one by one into my purse. "1, 2, 3, 4, 5." I hold the last one up for him to see. *It's my special blank bullet for stubborn asses like yourself.* "And one for my version of Russian roulette." I put it in the chamber and spin it.

I never carry a fully loaded revolver. I only carry 5 real bullets and one specially marked blank bullet. It keeps the gun on safety and is always there if I need to play Russian roulette. A trick I learned from the magician who works our crowds. Even if the odds fail and it ends up in the chamber, it won't hurt anyone as long as you are more than 5 feet away. It makes a real gunshot sound, so it takes a few moments before the victim realizes they haven't actually been shot.

Brad's eyes narrow again. He watches me as I reach down and pick up Max. I hand it to him. He takes it with his free hand, but he still doesn't put it on. I point to it and his cock with the gun, but he only licks his lips. His eyes dare me. *The adrenaline junkie.*

I lick mine too. My eyes flare wide, crazy, as I point the gun at his foot and pull the trigger. His foot jerks back instinctively as his eyes narrow into a straight line. His erection softens as his adrenaline spikes. *Now I have your attention.* The combination of the cock ring and the Viagra keep him from deflating altogether. "Brad, I don't take no shit from nobody. Remember when I told TD that earlier? Well, it's true. Rules are rules. You agreed to allow me to give you a Fucking Fantasy. This is what I choose for you. Now, what's it gonna be? Comply or be disciplined? What are you going to do, Brad?" I raise my eyebrows at him.

He doesn't answer.

I pull the trigger again. The sound of the dry click makes him shudder, but he doesn't put Max on. I hold up two fingers. "No? Let's see how Bella is doing over here. She seems to be enjoying herself."

As I walk over to where she lays, I see that Darren has turned the light off in the corner. *I hope I don't have to discipline him too for breaking the rules. If he has fucked up Angela's orgasm, there will be hell to pay.*

Bella is sliding the Nora in and out as she moans bringing herself to orgasm slowly. Pointing the gun at her foot, I turn to look at Brad smirking and immediately pull the trigger. He flinches visibly and frowns. I hold up three fingers.

He looks pissed, annoyed and horny as he strokes his cock until it is erect again. I give him a big, sweet smile as he slides the Max on. Immediately, he looks confused and surprised. The machine is fucking him. His eyes look up to my face and I point to Bella. She is fucking herself with slow, deep thrusts, then fast short jabs. Brad smirks at me when he figures out that they are connected. I watch as his eyes roll back in his head enjoying the remote fucking. When she turns on the vibration, he says out loud. "FUCK!" He slides Max off then thrusts himself deep into it over and over.

Bella feels his thrusts. "Fuck me! FUCK YEAH! HOLY FUCK! SEARY!" She collapses laughing back on the couch. "Whew! That was intense!" She turns it off while she rests.

Brad says to me as I walk back up to him, smiling. "Fuck me!"

"That's what I was trying to tell you." I put the gun back in my purse, then lay my hand on his shoulder as I walk around him. I give him a couple of friendly pats, then back away to survey the Fucking Fantasies I have created tonight.

Bella revs up the action again and Brad slips his blindfold back on letting out a long, low moan. *He isn't bored now.*

Mandy is on top of TD fucking his brains out while she thrusts the Joystick in her mouth then in his. They suck Charlie's cock together but have eyes

266

only for each other as Charlie watches feeling every lick and thrust the Joystick delivers, shouting to them. "Faster, Bitches, Faster, Fuck me! Fuck yeah!" When she jumps off TD's cock and spins around taking TD in her mouth to suck, she drops the Joystick unattended on the floor. As she lowers herself onto TD's face for him to devour her, Charlie screams. "Fuck me! Fuck me! What the fuck? Fuck me!" But they can't hear him for the headsets. Freebird is reaching frenzy fucking speed and she is giving TD the best head of his life as she mashes her pussy in his face and he buries it deep in her. Charlie watches, stroking himself.

Looking over at Rosa and Mac, she is off the Sybian and using the base as a step stool. She is kissing and licking Mac's abs moving up to his chest. I can't hear what she is saying but her expression is soft, not harsh and his python is standing out full and hard.

As I turn my attention to Darren and Angela, I walk closer to see what's happening in the dark. *Well, I'll be damned! That was Angela's problem.* Darren has her bent over the Sybian and is shoving his cock in her ass, fucking her anally while pulling her hair back. Her legs are quivering with each thrust he makes and when he spanks her ass, she bows up, then moans loud! "AH, FUCK ME!" He pounds and pounds her. Each time he spanks her, she bows up and moans. Then she surprises me, as she takes the Sybian dildo and tries to put it in her pussy for double duty. But Darren's hold on her hair keeps her from being able to manage it.

He realizes what she wants. "Fuck yourself baby!" He releases her hair.

Her head droops forward as she finds her vagina and masturbates while he holds his cock deep in her ass, waiting and watching. She thrusts and her face takes on the "O" expression, then she shouts. "FUCK ME, DARREN, FUCK ME!" He takes her hips and slides himself in and out her back door while she does the same with the dildo in the front. And finally, she has the orgasm she has been denied. Finally, she cums in convulsive spasms as she shouts my name with each mind blowing wave of her first orgasm. "SEARY, SEARY, SEARY." Then she slumps over the Sybian and Darren reaches around her hugging and stroking her hair.

Everyone is happy! Walking to the counter, I pull out TD's Porsche key and put it down. While I replace the bullets in my gun, TD, Mandy and Charlie all shout "Seary" close together. Followed by, Angela again shouting. "Seary, Seary, Seary!" And Darren shouting "Seary" too. *Time to go.* I take the bluetooth earpiece out and set it on the counter next to the Porsche key. Then I smile up at the camera in the corner and blow them a kiss as I exit. Running down the steps and over the veranda, I hear Mac's "Oh ... Seary!" When I'm past the infinity pool and entering the gardens, I hear Brad shout. "GORILLA!" Laughing, I raise my arms in the air. "Siri, you beautiful woman, you led them ALL to victory!" *Orgasm is truly a beautiful gift.*

Walking, skipping and trotting, I sing "Happy" and dance it as I stay on the path that Brad said led to the Golf Course. Once the initial high wears off, I slow down to walk and enjoy the flowers. They are so pretty and the late night is so clean and peaceful. As I walk, I let my guard slip. As soon as I do, I feel the isolation and loneliness start to creep over me. It makes me shudder. *I bring so much undeniable happiness to others. It really makes it tough to go home alone to an empty house.* I fold my arms under my breasts and give myself a reassuring hug. *You won't always be lonely. You'll find someone. Maybe it will be Moore.* Aurei's beautiful face floats into my mind. *No pity party now. Stay strong. Be grateful. You live a life most people only dream of, and people love you for it. You have real fans. You just made 9 people very happy. You rock! YES, I DID! YES, I DO! YES, I WILL!*

I step out onto the Golf Course and look up to the stars. *You know what? It's a Goodnight for a run.* Slipping my shoes off, I lift my purse strap up and over my head and start to jog to the Club house. The grass is soft on my feet and the feel of it, as I put one foot down then the other, gives me peace. *Running always clears my head.* I reach the clubhouse quickly.

When I get there, I am thrilled to find there is a party going on inside one of the banquet rooms. Cars fill the parking lot and there are a few taxi cabs waiting. Creeping as close as I can without being seen, I step into the fountain to clean my feet pretending to be drunk. I stagger to the first cab and get in, pull the door shut and lay on the seat. The driver puts his phone down. "Are you alone?"

"Yes, I'm leaving the bastard here. Go. Quick."

"Yes ma'am." When we are on the road back to town, he asks. "Where to Miss?"

"Drop me off at the gate of Dogwood Court please."

"Yes ma'am."

I slip my shoes back on thinking about Aurei. Leaning my head back, I close my eyes to rest. *Finally, I can focus on the Golden God.*

"Miss, Miss. Are you ok?" Someone is shaking me. "We are here. I can take you to the door if you have had too much to drink."

I open my eyes to see the taxi driver with the door open, leaning over me. "Shit!" I jump and recoil from his touch. "Where am I?"

He laughs and stands back up outside the cab door. "Dogwood Court, Ma'am."

"I must have fallen asleep. No, no. This is good. I will walk up." I dig in my purse and pull out a $100. "Keep the change. And don't tell anyone where you took me."

He sees the $100 and grins. "Your secret is safe with me."

OTHER BOOKS
By
Jessika Klide

Siri's Saga:
*****

UNTOUCHABLE: The Cocktail Party (Part 1)
UNTOUCHABLE: More of Moore (Part 2)
UNTOUCHABLE: The Stallion and Ruth (Part 3)
******

UNTOUCHABLE, Book 1 (Full version)
UNSTOPPABLE, Book 2
UNDONE, Book 3
Available in paperback at your local bookstore as a special order item.
Available in paperback and ebook on Amazon.com.
*****

UNTOUCHABLE, Book 1 (Full version)
Available on audiobook at Audible.com or Amazon.com.
******

Book 4 will be UNFORGETTABLE!
Releasing 2016

ACKNOWLEDGEMENTS

Without my husband, my soulmate, my Golden God, this book would never have been written. To him, I am eternally grateful. He continues to inspire me.

To my family, whose patience and critical input helped me stay the course. To them, hugs and kisses.

Special thanks to my BFF, who listened to the raw storyline and helped with the creation of the final plot.

To the advance readers, who volunteered to read a story from an unknown author, who tweaked sentences and thought lines perfectly and offered their honest critiques, then gave me what I so desperately needed to hear: Praise, a thousand years of thank yous!

To Maria Clark, End Solutions Inc., who edited the finished product. A big shout out. THANK YOU!

To JC Mason & Kristen Wetherbee, the cover models. You are, both, gorgeous!

To my fans, it is truly an honor to share my story with you!

YOURS TRULY!

JK

ABOUT THE AUTHOR

Jessika Klide is a pen name and she explains the reason why this way. "I'm from LA ... Lower Alabama. The Deep South! Since I write erotic romance, and my mind is super slutty, it's just better to use a pen name. Trust me on this! ;)"

Jessika's chosen genre is New Adult Erotic Romance and the basis of the stories she writes about are hot alpha males who love her strong, sexy, smart, fun and flirty women. Military men make her swoon because the love of her life, her happily ever after, was an Army helicopter pilot, who she proudly admits is her high school sweetheart. Yes. She fell in love at first sight! Her stories are about true love, with lots of kinky erotica sprinkled throughout and more than one happy ending. She and her hero have raised two beautiful boys. Cowboys also do it for her, because she grew up wearing cowboy boots and riding horses.

She is active on social media sites, so check her out. She welcomes her fans with real Southern Hospitality, so chat her up. She's talkative and loves to interact with her friends.

A NOTE TO THE READER

Because Siri Wright is a dancer, there are songs sprinkled throughout her story. They have been chosen specifically, not only for their music, but also for their lyrics, which are governed by strict copyright laws restricting the use in books.

It is certainly not necessary to listen to the music to enjoy Siri's Saga, but if you choose to, you will enhance your enjoyment and have a fuller, deeper understanding of Siri's heart.

All playlists for Siri's Saga can be found on my YouTube channel in the order they appear in the stories

Made in the USA
Charleston, SC
04 May 2016